THE WOMAN IN THE MIRROR

MIRROR

A Young Woman's Journey

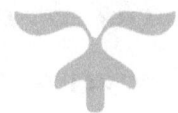

MARCH 1, 2018

WRITTEN BY RUTH DYKSTRA DEICHSEL

The content contained here-in

is creative non-fiction and is the story of a life of a young woman, a wife and of a mother's reflection. Researched and felt by the author. These contents are a work of Creative Non-Fiction

Table of Contents

BITS AND PIECES

Sharing some of the memories that I had been told. To begin, I'll start with some of my history before I had been born. As these events had taken place many years before. As it was documented by my ancestors and passed on through generations and now re-told in story form.

Going back to the year of 1914 in Oklahoma. It had been a very dry year. The drinking water, that there was, had to be taken from a cistern. Thus, bringing typhoid fever to several families and even to my ancestors. Typhoid Fever is when drinking water and even food have been contaminated by bacteria or pollution of some kind. Those were some very sad days for so many. Now they were just memories of family stories. Some of the families recovered and some were lost to this fever, which those folks would have had a very severe case of this fever.

It was in March of 1915, and it had been my Uncle Tom (my father's brother) and my father himself. The two of them with both of their families had boarded a train to Miles City, Montana. Here they only had stayed long enough to purchase what was needed for homesteading. This was to include a cow, a team of horses and a wagon. This was to carry them and their personal belongings of what they had, traveling north of Miles City then crossing the Yellowstone River, which at that time was called Dawson County.

It had been recorded that both families had spent the first few months here. Setting up a tent for shelter, as this would only be temporary. When there was a hard rain and with a windstorm, this had caused their tent to flood. Back in those days, we knew that the floor of the tent was the ground. So, it was that the tent need to be on much higher ground if at all possible. I had heard years later that the folks that had tried homesteading, were called squatters. So much of my past I was just beginning to learn about and even understand. With so much more to be told and the understanding of; what was my history in the years before I was born. It was my father and my Uncle who had decided to take the wagons and travel 300-400 miles to the Dakota's to look for work. They had not returned until sometime in October of that year. It had been about a 3-month journey before they were to return.

It was my grandmother, my great aunt and also my mother. Each of them had become mid-wives for each other, already having 3 children between them. (If I recall this correctly; one being my brother, who was born in 1915 and he was to be my only brother. He was born in the tent, while my parents were trying to homestead). The families were at this location for almost six months. At which time, upon the return of my Father and Uncle they had begun building a one-room sod home. My Mother was pregnant again during this time. Our one-room dug-out home had never quite got finished, so what was my family at that time, had moved into the dug-out home of my Aunt and Uncle. As it was, by this time there were, four adults and five children for about six months.

It was sagebrush in those days that was used for burning, as wood was extremely hard to come by. Gathering up this sagebrush and retrieving plenty for the time of being needed for burning was quite an undertaking most days.

It was in 1917 when Uncle Tom and my Father with both of their families, (about 20 people in all) had packed up their wagons from their last homestead and moved to work on the railroad near Miles City, Montana. This was close to 100 miles away. Though hopes were high, there still remained some anxiety as a new beginning for all was about to take place.

It was in this year of 1917, that unknowingly to them that this was the year that a severe drought had begun.

In 1919, fifty percent of all farmers trying to homestead had lost their land over the next several years.

Being born in Butler, Oklahoma in 1930. As this was before the great Dust

Bowl hit our state and it was recorded in history that so many surrounding states had felt the effects of the drought. This was a devasting disaster and had hit twenty-seven states in total. As it has been told, the Dust Bowl terror was to last until the year   1940.

Moving the years forward and recalling the winters that had laid several inches of this freshly fallen white blanket down on the homestead. Snow had covered every branch of every tree and covered the fields in its blanket of white. It was to lay heavily, where it had chosen to rest. The fields had a crisp blanket of white, that not even a blade of grass was to be seen until Spring.

After what felt like several months, Spring had arrived, bringing with it, new life to the surrounding fields and to the tree lined mountains. Our home was simple, but we managed with what we had. As others were struggling as we were, we were happy to be together. Yet, with the onset of Spring's arrival, there were to be new beginnings that we could feel positive about.

TIME OF INNOCENCE

Where does one begin when recalling of one's self, or of one's close to your own heart? Thoughts take you on a journey you haven't traveled in quite some time, or maybe you have, yet only in your mind. How far back should you go, or how far do you really want to go? As a young child, you see things differently than others would see them. So, where in this, does the term 'reality' come from? Stepping back into a time of what my memory has seen and what my heart remembers.

Being a young girl and the only child still at home. Well like, life can't get complicated enough sometimes. As I see this person looking back at me, from the mirror that hangs on the wall of my childhood home. This young girl who is at the age 14 years. She recalls what used to be, what is and dreams of a future that she would only hope that it could be. Her hair is of golden blonde, just resting atop her shoulders. Pulling back her hair now, to keep it from falling into this oval shaped face. Only now, small strands escape to rest on the cheeks of this on-looker in the glass. I begin to wonder what is she really like? Who is this young person, reflecting back at me? Seeing her reflection, she is of average height, say; maybe 4'8 or maybe even 4'9. Slender and the look of young and beautiful innocence. Her complexion smooth and not at all aged; by what sometimes were the cold and harsh bitter winters, or the summers' bright rays of warmest sunshine. Her eyes almost appear blue, though others would say that they are, of a bluish green. The dress that she wears, has a few years of wear, yet fresh and crisp like the morning air. Not too short or too long, but just resting above the knee. The sleeves of this dress are capped, leaving room for her slender arms to move about freely. While her legs are long and slender, not quite shapely yet as are some, of the older girls she knows. Though, the calves show strength and muscle from daily walks, as well as from the undertaking of the daily responsibilities of chores.

Reflecting on my being born in southern, OK in 1930, the homestead of my grandparents. Being too young to remember my grandparents, though I would enjoy hearing the stories that others would tell. Our home was built of sod and having a dirt floor. Having only the essential rooms to make shelter for a few adults, and us young ones. At times, it was a bit overcrowded with children of young ages, though they managed as best they could. There sure had been quite the houseful and not a lot of room in those days.

Times were hard for the adults in this homestead, as well as children, yet time keeps moving forward. Everyone working together, as this was our home. Everyone seemed to be making plans for their futures. In which this, we knew then, was only temporary housing for us all.

It may have been when I was about the age of 5 years when we had packed up and moved to Watalula, Arkansas. Not really being able to recall for certain, though it may have been because my father had a land opportunity there. So, recalling with what had once been mentioned before, our belongings had been packed up with what we had, and we were all moving on to an unknown future they lay in wait for us all. Once, we had found our place, we began building of what was to be our home. It was hard work and each of us doing all that we could, to build this vision of what my parents had been creating in their minds. How it would turn out, I was not quite sure but needed to stay as positive as one so young, could be.

My thoughts are still adrift, as this person seems to be only a shadow now looking back at me. Where did those years go and yet, time still continues moving forward. As it seems to be, that time waits for no one. Not even for the young or for the old.

A person looks back at what once was; for all the memories that leads you to where you are now. For all the days, the years ahead, for the memories you haven't made yet. My life is just beginning, though I sometimes feel that I have already been through so much. Yet, there is a future out there, my future. Trying to live one day at a time. Making the best of every day that I have been given. Even those days that I wish I could take and start them over. Though if I were to do that, then everything else would change, and life would turn out differently and possibly not for the best. So, no more dwelling on what ifs' Life is a journey and here is part of mine.

REFLECTIONS

Moving my thoughts and memories into the year of 1940 and I, being at the age of 10 ten years now, and living in Watalula Arkansas, which is in Franklin County. Being, that I would be in the 5th grade, I no longer am attending school. I was no longer able to continue my schooling, as my father needed me here at home to help with the daily undertaking of taking care of our homestead. Any further schooling and learning would have to wait and maybe someday I will be able to learn what the other kids my age were already learning. I was extremely occupied with working as a farm hand for my father and mother. For now, my education would be what everyday life could teach me, and I would learn anything else as life went along. That is what I was being called, or as others would consider it; being a farm hand. Putting in nearly 60 hours a week, and this didn't include what would or could have been my schoolwork. I guess, no wonder I always felt so incredibly tired but knew that I needed to push myself through (what felt like never ending chores of this life, that had seemed to have been chosen for me.). It would strike me as it had, in prior days. Having had the feelings of my self-worth. I was born a girl – a daughter, not a boy or a son. Now, mind you I didn't have ill feelings about, my being of help to my parents. I was glad to help in any way, that they felt it necessary. Yet, I could not seem to overcome this feeling that I often felt, that my parents were wanting a son and not the daughter they had gotten. By this time, my two older sisters and my brother had already left home and now had lives of their own. There had been another older sister, though she had died before I was born. She had gotten lockjaw and had died at the age of three. As for my brother, he was much older than I, so yes, he too was gone from the home stead. He had moved to the state of Washington to look for work in the coal mines. Both sisters now living in Oklahoma at the time. My oldest sister had married when I was only 3 years old, so I didn't see her often, yet when she did come home to visit, she was absolutely wonderful to me. I really did relish in the thoughts of having an older sister. Now, not to say that my other older sister, her and I too, had a special bond that only sisters could have. It was a closeness that I felt when they were home, and a deep sadness when they had to leave. I missed them terribly and even being as young as I was, I knew that their place wasn't here, but I wished, that it did not have to be so different. I was growing up without them, and so many times throughout any given day, I just needed them here. Just to have your sisters close sometimes, is what I really needed.

I think they knew this too, though they knew that I couldn't come with them. For now, my place was here. Or at least it was for the time being, for however how long that would be. I would have faith that someday things would get better.

Early morning had come to this quaint little homestead of our home. But it was our home. A home that was built with hard working hands and a determined spirit.

I had awakened to the sounds of many birds singing and the bustling of movements outside. I lie awake listening to the echoes of the morning. The sun had just risen over the mountain peaks off in the distance. As with the morning dew, you could see it glistening off the blades of grass even far off into the distance of the fields that lay before the mountains. It laid like a blanket, shimmering at the foot of the Ozark mountains. It actually was a picture-perfect morning. Swinging myself up out of my bed, decided I better begin to start what was to be the beginning of another day. My mother already at the cook stove, preparing what was to be our breakfast, I was scrambling to gather my warm sweater that had been embroidered with flowers. It had become one my favorite sweaters when the air was still crisp against the morning dew. This I was doing while also attempting to tie my hair up and making it out the door to find where my father had gone.

Looking into the fields I had seen him off in the distance, too far for him to hear me call out his name. Well, I figured I'd better get the cows milked, gather the eggs, and get the hay pitched, while waiting on my mother to call for me, as my father would be back soon. The sun was shining a bit brighter now, it was getting to be a little later in the morning. With chores done, the cows are milked, eggs are gathered, hay for the horses and then the barn shoveled. I soon began smelling the aromas of fresh baking, coming from the inside our home.

Father was on his way back in and now he could see me greeting him, as his approach was now closer.

Not much time for relaxing, still had what seemed like an endless list to complete before my day would be considered done. Even though the warmness of the suns' rays felt warm against my face, I decided to keep my favorite sweater on; for going into the woods would be somewhat cooler. The sun was mostly hidden by the high towering trees, as I walked along the path. I could hear the bustling of the creek, just off in the distance. Waters rushing and flowing, it was like listening to a rhythm it had all its' own. Like it knew it was reaching for a place it had to be. It was as if the waters were dancing in the coolness of the morning. Observing the smaller animals as they were chasing each other about. It was like they were playing a game of hide and seek. Bringing my thoughts back now to the path I was on. I was now coming up on the vastly large area of black berries and next to them were raspberries. Grabbing a better hold of my two bulky buckets, with their thin handles, I began to pick those berries that seemed just to be waiting for me.

Now, I just couldn't help eating one or two. Tasting sweet and most pleasant, I decided to enjoy each and every one that had found its' way to me before they found their way into my bucket. Now, not realizing just how much time I had actually spent, but soon had those two buckets nearly overflowing. I guess, time to head back towards home, knowing that I would be needed there as well. There would be plenty for me to pick later when we would be wanting more. Providing that the birds and animals had not taken them for a meal for themselves. Yet, there were plenty so really, there was no need to have second thoughts on there being more later.

Being a Saturday morning, there were an awful lot of things to do. Sometimes, even if just for a few moments, would forget what day it actually was. Arriving home, the horses and mule had already been turned out into the pasture. Turning over the bucket of berries to my mother, I turned around and headed back outdoors.

Father was waiting for me, as he and I headed into the far field to pick rocks. This chore would take us the better part of the day. As this needed to be done before we could hitch the horse and plow for planting. We; my father and I were well prepared for our day. With us, we had plenty of cool water, a sandwich or two, a few pieces of fruit and freshly baked cookies for a snack. This would be mostly welcomed, in the later part of our day.

My father guided the horses in turning up the dirt in the field, while I followed close behind throwing the rocks onto the wagon until we nearly had enough of what would not put too much of a strain on the horses. Not to mention that I was tired and every muscle aching. This had taken us the better part of the day and it was decided that, with all that we had, this would be enough for the day. It was a good day's work. Even my father did smile and agreed it was time to head back towards home. It had to be nearly supper time, as the sun was getting lower in the sky and a cooler breeze was felt as the day was working its' way into the evening.

Father was unhitching the horses as I was washing off the days' dust and dirt and then meeting him in the barn to feed and settle the animals in for the night. All in all, it was a long-hot day, but feeling well satisfied that good things were accomplished today. And a soft smile came upon my face as my father touched my shoulder and told me, I was sure a good helper today.

It was nearly nightfall now, as the days' heat turned into a cooler and gentler breeze. It felt pleasant against my skin, closing my eyes as I stood here on our wooden porch. Feeling that gentle breeze as it brushed past me, as it combed through my hair. It was almost tempting to stay out on the weathered beaten porch and just enjoy the silence of nightfall. With discerning thoughts of what I had accomplished today, that it was a good days' work. Knowing that I had put in long hours today with my father and with the feeling of satisfaction, I stepped inside our home. My mother was in her favorite rocking chair and glanced up as I stepped inside. With a fire lowly burning in the fireplace, it was the sounds of the crackling of the wood that seemed to keep time with the creaking of the rocker as it rocked back and forth. Supper was still warm on the stove and I knew that I had plenty of an appetite. Quietly sitting and resting at the table, I enjoyed the simple yet filling meal my mother had prepared. Washing up the few dishes that I had, along with the feeling of contentment, that hadn't taken too long to do, which was a good thing, cause my weariness was starting to settle into my bones. Heating up a large bucket of water, I took this to my room, as this I would use to bathe in. Needed to just finish washing off the days' hard work and of course there was church in the morning.

The fire was nearly out now in the fireplace and only a few small pieces of wood that had been gathered, was giving off an ember glow which had provided a shadowy light in the dark, along with a few of the oil lamps that were still dimly lit.

Sunday morning seemed to arrive early. The sun streaming through the small version of what was my window, it was the start of another day. Feeling quite rested, I had decided it was best to put my feet on the floor and begin the start of what was to be my day.

As we; mother, father and myself were traveling down the dirt trodden road in my father's older pick-up, it was for all to hear, the melody of the church bells ringing, as if they were gently singing their welcome as many were arriving to the small church that sat just off a short distance from the road. Our church had been built from the timbers of the nearby woods of the Ozarks. The windows were of cut glass with the symbol of the cross etched into each of them. A tower that fit the church bell just perfectly, as if it were reaching to be higher than the treetops. It was rather quite beautiful for our small community. Yes, it was a very pleasant morning to be at church. Even if it was just for a short time, to leave all the chores and a lot of everything else behind and to just enjoy the pleasures of the morning. The singing was enjoyable as everyone seem to fit together just right. The smiling faces and welcoming greetings just made a person feel warm and content inside our own selves. Yes, this was a beautiful Sunday morning to remember.

There were many of our neighbors that I recognized, and some that I did not know. Though even the unknown faces seemed kind with the warm and gentle smiles they wore. I don't know if they were always this kind, but I would take it for what it was worth and just enjoy the company of their kindness.

THE CALL TO TRAVEL

Not real sure exactly, just how many months had passed; yet sometimes it felt like an eternity. Well, to me it was an eternity. Some would wonder of those thoughts. Though, I feel that it is in each ones' own mind of how they perceive the word, or what life's events led up to the feeling or thought of what an eternity is or was. I remember when I had once wondered, what exactly was my purpose here. On this earth, I mean. My mother seemed to grow more distant from me, though I was sure that she loved me and maybe had a hard time showing it, or maybe just didn't know how. She once told me that I had been a mistake and was supposed to have been born a 'boy'. Now, why would she say, such a thing. Didn't she know or even realize how those words cut like a knife into your soul. I really did love my parents, but wondered; why was I born a 'girl'? A girl she really didn't want. Is that maybe why, I worked so hard, sometimes harder than other girls my age should have been working. Now, don't misunderstand me, I realized and had come to terms with knowing that I was still needed. That I was needed to help with the responsibilities of helping my parents. I guess my ideas of helping and theirs, was or appeared to be so very different. This was a question that may not ever be answered.

It had been decided in the days that followed. That I would be taking a trip to spend some time at the home of my mother's sister. Not really sure why. Though, if I really stopped to think about it, I felt that I did know, yet I didn't really like much thinking the thoughts that I had. Started to think that maybe I had made my mother and father angry. So, angry that my mother had hardly spoken to me. I was so torn inside and became unconsciously quiet. What had I done? After all I guess, I even thought this idea that turned into a decision, was probably a good idea, on all of our parts. Still couldn't help feeling the emptiness that filled me. It was like falling into a dark hole and now, you were unable to see the bottom. A feeling that I was being discarded, like something they didn't want. Just maybe I was overreacting. Letting my thoughts and emotions run away in my head. I had at times wondered, have others ever felt this way, or was it just me? It had been decided that I would leave after early morning chores on the coming Saturday. It had given me at least a warm feeling inside, that I would be going to visit my Aunt and Uncle in Oklahoma and to see my cousins that I hadn't seen for quite some time. While I would be away, and when my Father needed help with the chores, there was a neighbor just down the road that had offered to help out while I was away. Almost felt a bit guilty for leaving, but it was not my choice and it would be best for now, for just a few months; through the summer, until school started up again, is what my father had told me. Though, I knew that my going back to school wasn't really what I would be doing. I would not be attending school, when I was to return before the start of the new school year once it had begun. I would continue to help on the farm when I returned from Aunt and Uncle's home in Oklahoma.

It was on the following Saturday morning, after I had helped with chores, that I had most of my belongings already packed. Upon leaving, my mother had not even said good-bye or wished me a safe travel. Not really sure of what I was expecting, but I guess I didn't think or didn't want to, that she wouldn't say anything at all. Father had taken me into town to catch the mid-morning bus. We spoke a little, just small talk mostly. Though he reassured me that everything would be okay, and that I would be home before too long. Looking over at him, all I could manage was a weak smile, though not much of a smile really. I had the feeling that, he may have known how I was feeling.

Outspoken feelings were not something any one was really used to, or was it practiced. So, I did as others did and was taught. And that was to keep what, you were feeling, good or bad to yourself. If in doing this, then who was there to talk to when you just needed someone to listen to you. That deep dip in the road had startled me and brought me back to the present, even though my mind was like a million miles away. Getting even closer to town now, I began to wonder what was in store for me when I arrived at Auntie's. I knew I would be happy to see her and Uncle. My cousins that I had not seen since last summer when they had last come to visit. Or had it been even longer than that? Not, really sure now; now that I thought about it for a bit. Anyway, I would do my best and make this time away from home as good as I possibly could, considering. Just a few hours from now, events were going to soon be changing.

Arriving now at the bus station, my father pulling up to the curb, putting the truck into gear, he had once more told me, not to worry that things would work out, and I would be home soon. Trying my best to understand and returning to him a faint smile, that even then, I was certain of his softer-spoken words to me. I really knew he meant well in his efforts to try and comfort my unspoken emotions. It was my own memories that were nagging me in my head. Would things really be alright, and work out for me in the end? Sometimes, I felt like I was being packed and shipped off like something that was no longer needed and was just getting in the way of other things. Though, I knew there were things; things that I was not being told about. Though, I guess time would soon tell, and whatever was to happen, will happen. I just knew that I needed to believe in my most inner self, that things will turn out to be alright. Had to have faith, the faith that I could not see, yet knew it was still there; somewhere.

My father stayed with me, long enough to see me off at the bus stop. My bus was approaching soon, and I still needed to check in and grab my ticket. For now, this was going to be a one-way ticket. Resting for a bit on the bench that was provided, I sat with my suitcase close to me. My father decided to sit with me, until the bus arrived. I was grateful for his company, not knowing how long it would actually be, before I would be seeing him and my mother again. Not sure just how much time had passed if I were to guess maybe an hour or so. Before awfully long, the bus appeared down the street and people were gathering at the edge of the walkway now, awaiting for its' arrival. My father stood, and I followed suit, picking up my suitcase and making my way towards the small crowd that began to gather. As I waited, my father placed his hands on my shoulders, and he had bent down to give me a kiss on my forehead and gave me a hug. For the first time in a long time, longer than what I could remember, he told me that he 'Loved Me" and for me to mine my manners with Aunt and Uncle. Those softly spoken words, I will cherish them forever. Papa: I said, I love you too and I will mine my manners. I will make you proud of me Papa. My eyes started to glisten as tears began to well up in my eyes.

Papa knew, without my even saying anything more. One more hug from Papa and I was walking the steps to get onto the bus. My father had waited for me to take my seat. Making sure to take a window seat, I could see my father following me with his eyes as I found my seat on the bus. He waved a good-by to me and I kept waving even as the bus pulled away and my father faded as the bus kept moving down the street. As I settled into my seat, I had plenty of time for thinking. Staring out the window and not really seeing anything, I was remembering the past few hours with my father and how those precious moments with him had made me feel.

Almost feels like, it was a lifetime ago. Not sure, just how much time had passed, yet when the bus began to brake hard, I had looked up to see that the bus had stopped suddenly and was letting some cows cross the roadway. Seemed like they may have wandered off from a field close by somewhere. All following one another. Where could they all be going? This had quickly brought my mind back from the memories that had overtaken me, just moments earlier.

Must have been late in the afternoon when the bus arrived at the depot. Everyone aboard was beginning to gather their things as the bus was coming to its' final stop. I sat waiting for most everyone to exit and then slowly rising up to take my place in line. Being almost the last one to exit this bus, except for a young couple that chose their seat at the very back of the bus. My one and only suitcase would be given to me, once I was completely off the bus.

It was still a bit warm for this time of day. Though shadows were beginning to cast themselves off buildings and even off the people that were passing by.

I eagerly looked for familiar faces. It was like looking into a large crowd, hoping to catch a glimpse of the sweet face that I knew and remembered. It sure was the best and the sweetest; of surprises, not only was my Aunt at the station; meeting my arrival, but there was also my Uncle and also two of my cousins, one of which was closest to my age. They were eagerly awaiting, for the arrival of the bus to pull into the depot. Seeing them through the small square of the window, I had wanted to reach over to put my hand up to the glass to wave hello to them. Though, I could only wave to them from where I stood. It sure did feel good, to see them smiling and waving back. It helped me to forget the painful ache my heart was feeling.

As I waited my turn in line to exit the bus, there was such a quiet that came over everyone, a strange kind of thing, no one pushing or hollering, and it actually made, me feel a bit more grown up than I was in my years.

As I stood there on the walkway; just looking at everything around me, I heard someone call my name. Turning in the direction of the voice that I heard, someone had said my name again only a bit louder this time. Then catching the face behind the voice, I quite loudly called back. What a happy sight to see. Forgetting everything else, just for a moment, my heart beat faster, and I could not control the smile that came upon my face. My cousin Ellie was sure a welcomed sight. As I saw her, then I also saw my Aunt, my Uncle and Dessa. Ellie and Dessa were just a couple of years older than myself. Though, I remember them quite well. Their older sisters could not make it, but I would still possibly see them sometime during my stay. They too, were older and did not live at home. So, I understood that there would be a chance that I might not be seeing them on this visit.

THE INTERVIEW

Well, I gathered up all my belongings and with the help of Uncle, we put everything in Uncle's truck. As we were now headed towards their home. There was now a gentle breeze that blew, and it felt so very nice against my face. The sun hadn't quite set, as it was rather early in the day for it to be doing that. Looking around at my cousins, they too were enjoying the late afternoon breeze. Exchanging smiles, we immediately started catching up on the past and what we all had been doing. We did have many memories and we were soon to be making more. How much better could that be? I was feeling content and happy at the moment.

It didn't seem like an awfully long trip to Aunt and Uncle's home. Time passed rather quickly and even rather nicely. Though I still thought of Papa and his ride back to our home, he was driving back alone, and my thoughts were now with him.

Well, settling in was good and sharing a room with Ellie wasn't so bad either. She said she was happy to have the company, and I promised that I wouldn't get in her way and that I would be a good roommate for her. All settled in now and went to see Aunt Nellie, looking to help her out and start earning my keep. She was tending to start supper and I was looking to help. With now having an extra mouth to feed and I did not want to be a burden to them.

It was a nice gathering at the table for supper. The windows were still open, allowing for the gentle breeze of the early evening in. Good conversation with family was always a comfort to the heart. Recalling the day's events and what exactly would be my role; now that I was here. Well, here I would be, at least until school started up again in the fall. Along, with my being able to help out here, in any way that I could. I also wanted to help earn money that would also help with my stay here. Aunt Nellie, spoke of job in town that maybe I could do. Now, this particular job; I had no experience in, but everyone had to start somewhere, right? And the only way to gain experience, is to start at something you haven't yet done. I decided to go into town the next morning and see about this job. For me, I'm not always outspoken, sometimes a little shy but would need to overcome that in a hurry. Though, I knew that I was polite, respectful and I really did like helping other people. So, it was settled then, I would start out early after breakfast and was to walk the few miles into town. Cousin Ellie and Dessa would walk with me in the morning, as they had a few things that they also wanted to take care of. There wasn't any use in resisting their offer. Of course, I was sure glad to have the

company, so I didn't refuse their offer
of company and of friendship. I don't
think it would have done me any good to
object. It was settled without too much
discussion. I was to have company
while I walked, but it was good all the
same. It was a beautiful morning in late
June, walking along the roadway with
your two best cousins, who were more
like sisters. We walked, talked, and
laughed. So many things to share with
each other, no matter what the day had
in store for us, we all agreed that it was
the first of many good days for all three
of us. It sure did enlighten my heart to
be with them. It seemed that some of
the pains that my heart was feeling
days before, had been lifted some and
this had given me the feeling of a much

brighter outlook of what my days or even months could be like. I still had a way to go, but some things were getting better, and I was incredibly grateful for that.

Coming into town now, we were approaching my stop. Ellie and Dessa, wishing me good luck and told me that I did look nice and even grown up, so not to worry, I would do just fine. Well, this was my very first interview for a job; a job that actually would pay me, for working. I was so nervous and really hoping that it didn't show too much. Ellie and Dessa, would be back to pick me up in about an hour. Didn't think it would take that long, but one never really knows.

Once inside, I looked about, and this place was bigger than I had imagined. I guess, not really knowing what to expect, but somehow this was more than what I would have thought. This was a big department store with a café/restaurant inside. There were plenty of people, both young and old alike. Some were shopping and there were some sitting at tables and at the counter, which was located to the far left.

While I was looking over this place, a woman with long dark hair had come up to me. Of course, she was older than me, but she was young in comparison to some of the others. Her hair tied back away from her face. Yet, her face was gentle, and it matched her voice when she spoke. She introduced herself as Miss Gretta. She seemed as if she knew why I was there. I introduced myself and told her that I would like to apply for the waitress job that I was told was available. We spoke at great lengths about what the job would entail and what my responsibilities would be. Knowing that I had no experience, yet I was an awfully hard worker, and would go over and beyond of what was expected of me. Miss Gretta told me, she would be training me and felt that I would do just fine. We went over the hours and even what I would be paid each hour. It wasn't much, but I could earn even more by days' end. Making tips that the customers would leave, for my service to them in serving them drinks and food. This was like a whole new world to me, one that I had never experienced, and it would soon change. I would make sure that I succeeded in this new part of my young life. It would surely be something, that someday I would look back on and have fond memories of. Before, Miss Gretta and I were through, she had shown me where the uniforms were kept and which one, I would be assigned. I could change at work when I arrived for my shift. I think Miss Gretta and I would get along nicely. Even though, she was my trainer, she and I became friends that day and she would help me along the way, as I needed it. I thanked her for her time, her patience and understanding. I would start in two days.

Standing just outside the front door now, of this large department store and café/restaurant and feeling very well pleased with how things had gone. The name of this large department store and café/restaurant was called; Kresge's. There were a few of these large stores, but I didn't know the location of all of them.

Waiting now for Ellie and Dessa, it wasn't too long of a wait. As they approached, they must have known how things had gone, just by the look on my face. It must have given them every clue they needed. They were smiling and excited to hear how things had gone. I started to tell them everything as we walked. I told them about Miss Gretta and how big that store was. They could hear the excitement in my voice as I spoke. Wouldn't Aunt Nell and Uncle be pleased. The time traveled quickly as we headed back towards home. Aunt Nell, I think must have spoken with Miss Gretta ahead of my coming to stay, as she already had known why I was there. All in all, it was okay because, I knew Aunt Nell knew more than what I would have thought about my situation. She had a very kind heart and treated me like I belonged. That made me feel very warm inside and pushed those sad feelings way to the back of my mind and heart. Right now, they had no place in taking part of how I felt just now. I felt very eager to tell her and Uncle how my day had gone and when I would be able to start.

Getting settled in and having a chance to reflect on the days' events, couldn't help feeling just a bit excited that at the same time, brought on a tinge of fear. Now, this fear was nothing like being afraid of the dark or having the sense of falling when there was no one to catch you. This maybe was just the anticipation of the not knowing. It was not really a bad thing. Looking at it, as a step into an adult world. Not really an adult yet myself, but I think I was emotionally growing up like one.

Aunt Nell and Uncle were pleased and very happy for me, and they encouraged me in giving me the confidence push, that I may have needed. I had the assurance of Ellie and Dessa, that I would be a good fit and that I would do very well. I would start this new chapter of my life at the start of the new week. Decided to write my Mom and Pa a letter and let them know how I was getting along. Hoping that they too, would be proud that I found a way to help out, not just doing daily chores, but contributing in other ways as well. Even though, things were much different back at home, I still wanted them to be proud of me, even though there were many times I really didn't know or felt like they were proud of me, or even wanted me around. Maybe, this would help a little, in changing them on how they felt, or maybe just her; I should say. Well, finishing off this letter, I did feel good in writing to them, so down to the roadside mailbox I went. It was quite a long driveway, yet tonight I did not mind. The distance to the edge of the driveway was a chance for me, just to capture the current days' events and just to clear my head. All in all, it was a good thing.

Time sure does seem to pass quickly. The summer was nearly over and almost time for me to think about what it was going to be like once I was to arrive back at home.

My time working in the diner, gave me a whole new way of thinking about things and maybe even about people. Met some interesting people, some who would gather just to catch up on the daily gossip or how they would be spending the rest of their day. Some were shoppers, while others were travelers just passing through. This was an awakening experience for me, just to see how other people got along with each other and even to strangers that they had only encountered, even just briefly. It felt like this was or maybe could be a new chapter for me. Just was not really sure where this would take me. Though, I could say that this was something new in my life, and it wasn't a bad thing. Very possibly, a steppingstone into whatever else may lie ahead.

Sitting now on the edge of my bed, in the room that I shared with Ellie, I was remembering all the different things that had happened, that had led me up to where I am now. I guess, there were so many things, some wonderfully good, and some that had made me feel like I was still living in limbo. Really couldn't dwell on those things for too terribly long, wasn't sure that I wanted to re-live those events. At least, not for very long anyway.

There was a knock at the door, bringing me out of the memory trance I found myself caught up in. It was Ellie, not wanting to disturb me, yet she was so excited, she could hardly catch her breath. Then finally sitting down next to me, she excitedly needed to tell me; she had something for me. Ellie knowing that it was only a matter of weeks, before I had to head back home to Arkansas, she handed me a piece of paper. I could see it was folded several times. I looked at her with questions in my eyes, not knowing exactly what was in that folded piece of paper. As for Ellie, she had such a smile on her face, that it couldn't help being brought out in her eyes. With shaking fingers, I began to unfold this piece of paper, still looking at her with questioning eyes. "Please, just open it, and then I'll explain" Ellie said. Opening up this mysterious piece of paper, held the name of a man. A man's name, that Ellie had acquired. Ellie had proceeded to tell me that I should write to this man and get to know him. She explained that she knew that things were exceedingly difficult for me at home, and maybe that writing to him, might help ease my feelings of not really being wanted at home. (It seemed like, so many people knew why I was really here). What had my mother really said about me, to my Aunt, Uncle and then now my cousins seemed to know too. I was not completely certain that I even knew the real reasons. No one ever came out and really told me. What I thought, was in my own mind, but so many different things had led me to believe that what I was feeling, was true, or was it?

I accepted this secret gift from Ellie, though not yet certain when I would begin writing to this man or even if I would. This particular man, he had served in the war and from what I understood, a lot of his time was spent overseas. I was told that he was a bit older than myself, though maybe writing him, I could acquire a new friend. Good friends were always good to have. For now, I'll tuck away this gift from Ellie, and keep it in a safe place. For now, this was our secret and a secret that not anyone will ever know about.

Hearing Aunt Nellie, calling us from the kitchen, we both had made a commitment; giving each other a big hug, I told her that no matter what happens, I do love her dearly, more like a sister and that we would for what we knew, no matter where we ended up in this life, we would always keep in touch.

Hurrying down the short hallway to the kitchen, Aunt Nellie, Uncle Harden, and Dessie were patiently waiting for the two of us to arrive. Ellie and I both at the same time, apologized for keeping them waiting and took our places at the table. Aunt Nellie looked at me and then at Ellie, and asked if everything was alright? We both smiled and answered with; "Everything was just fine". Conversation was delightful, as we all shared what our day had been like. (Except for the secret that was Ellie's and mine).

The days had turned into just a few short weeks. They seemed to have passed by so quickly. So much has happened in such a short time, almost made me wonder if it was actually me, who had been living it. I would actually be leaving for my own home in Arkansas by the end of the following week. Only had a few more days left at the diner before my job would end there as well. I had met and made some friends their too, that would always stay with me in my mind. The experiences there, would only make me stronger. I was growing up, not just in years but in life experiences as well. The time that each day held, seemed to pass by even more quickly, than it had the day before. The day was finally arriving when I would be back on a bus headed for home. Having mixed feelings now; Did I really want to go back? Sure, I missed my father and even my mother, I guess. Sounds kind of cruel, but it was something that I had to figure out and after all, she was my mother. I did love her of course, but not the way a heart aches for the longing of someone you deeply miss. I learned a lot, being away these few months. Aunt Nellie and Uncle Harden, along with my cousins were also my family. They helped me through a lot, letting me into their home and making me feel, like I belonged some place. I will always feel a very special love for them, for that. Then the morning came much too quickly, as there was only a day left to be here before the day of my departure. Waking early, as not to miss the beautiful sunrise. I was mostly packed now and just waiting, waiting for time. Sometimes, that was the most difficult part, the waiting.

Being careful, as not to wake the others, I thought I would just step outside into the coolness of the morning. Aunt Nellie was already awake and moving about in the kitchen. She turned and gave me a memorable smile, and with a loving greeting of "Morning", which was like sunshine. Stepping out onto the wooden porch, looking out as far as the eye could see, it brought back memories of when I had done this very same thing, before I had left home to come here. The view of course was different, yet the same in many ways. Strange isn't it, how certain things allow you to realize moments and feelings of other places, at a different time of your life? How something you are now doing, feels like the same thing you had once, done before. Those feelings were bitter-sweet, and soon; it would be again. I would; once more be on a bus headed back in the direction, I had once come from only a few short months ago.

There was more movement now, coming from inside the house, the home that was mine; only if it was temporary. Hearing the others, talking, and rustling about, I went back inside. Offering my help to Aunt Nellie and it gave me an inner peace, to feel that comfortable with them.

Helping Aunt Nellie now, with putting our breakfast on the table, everyone began taking their places around the long wooden table that Uncle Harden had built years ago.

Everything was smelling wonderful. There was so much food, Aunt Nellie had out done herself this morning. She had for as long as I could remember, had always enjoyed baking and cooking. And today was one of those special days. With prayers and blessings said, we all dug into such a wonderfully prepared breakfast. Conversation was very pleasant this morning, I myself, was telling Aunt Nellie and Uncle Harden, how grateful I was, that they had allowed me to come and stay with them for a while. It was more than just a visit to me. It had given me the opportunity to see so many things, to see those things so differently, then what I had thought they might have been. It was a chance for me to get to know them better, and I would always take their love and kindness, with me forever.

Time was getting to be towards the mid-morning, when it was decided that we would all go on a picnic down by the lake. One last get-together for us, before I had to take the next day's bus back home. It was a splendid idea and we started to prepare ourselves for that. With all the preparations complete, we had started out for our favorite picnic spot down by the lake. As it was, this time of late morning, the lake was quiet; nothing now but the rippling of the water. The trees were heavy with leaves and offered us shade. Gentle breezes that seemed calm, had given us a very tranquil feeling. My thoughts had drifted, taking me to a place of how I missed such precious moments with Ma and Pa. Though, then I was much younger, yet still a warming memory. I could feel the warm sensation that wanted to build up in my eyes but knew this would not be the best of times for that. What I had longed for and what really was; was so very the opposite. I knew that I needed to make the best of things, even if it made my insides ache. The sound of my name had brought me back to the present, and the others had taken up in conversation, and were addressing me. Apologizing for the wandering of my mind, I happily became a part of their discussion. Yet, they all seemed to know where my thoughts had taken me. Aunt Nellie and Uncle Harden wanted to be sure that I knew that they, very much had enjoyed my being able to stay with them. I was a big help to them and at the same time I had grown up in just a few short months. I had taken on a job that I had no experience in and now I knew what it was like, to be a part of the group of people that worked and brought home a paycheck. It was not much, but I had earned it and it made me feel good to be able to contribute and be part of something that had helped the ones I love, even if it wasn't a whole lot.

Aunt Nellie and Uncle Harden knew that times were hard and even heart-breaking for me at home. Even though Aunt Nellie was my mother's sister, she knew how; out of place, I had been feeling for quite some time. She at several times, had told me I would always be welcomed in their home and would always have a place to stay. It would be a 2nd home for me, is what she had told me. Looking up and meeting her loved filled eyes and soft smile, couldn't help but smile a bit myself through the glaze of tear-filled eyes. In many ways I didn't want to leave here, it was a feeling of belonging and of being wanted. Yet, knowing that this was only temporary, I would be back again someday to visit. This is what my heart and mind were telling me. I didn't know for sure what would lie ahead in my future. I wanted most of all to keep in touch with the people, my family, that I had come to care so much about; the more time I spent with them, all this time it was priceless.

It was early in the evening now and had decided to rest a bit on the front porch swing. Gently gliding back and forth on the swing, feeling at times that I too, had become like a permanent fixture here on this porch. The sun was beginning to set, giving the sky an unbelievably beautiful amber glow. The clouds that were once white during the day, had now the appearance of gentle blues and soft pinks. This would be a sunset to remember.

Ellie had come out from the screened door to see where I had gone. She then paused before she had come to join me and we sat together in the swing, first not saying anything, just swinging. I was the one to speak first and just like that; so, had she. We just looked at each other and started to laugh. Laughter was something I had not heard in quite a while when I was at home. The laughter felt good when it was coming from the heart. Then, when I started talking, she listened very tentatively. I wanted her to know, how much I appreciated her. Being like a sister to me, it meant the world to me, to have someone close to your own age to talk to. I mean really talk to. Ellie had also agreed and had said how glad she was to have me there, spending time with her and the family.

Soon, Ellie began talking about this man's name she had given me. She was curious as to when I thought, I would start writing to him. I wasn't really sure, I told her. Though writing him still did sound intriguing. So that, had started me thinking about this man again. When would I find time to write to him? So many thoughts now, of how I would even begin to do that. We must have talked and shared so many things, as now the sun had disappeared, and the moon now gave way to its' night light. Only this bright moon and so many bright stars gave way to the dark that outlined the night sky. Deciding that we should now head back inside, as we then could visit with the rest of the family. As tomorrow would begin another day. The day that I would be heading back home, to once again be with my mother and father. I really was having mixed feelings about going back. Though that was my home, even if it were uncomfortable at times. Not, letting that bring me down, I would be just as helpful as before and after all they were my parents and I did love them, in spite of everything else.

Morning had come too quickly, is what I had thought while hearing voices outside this bedroom door. Was sure glad to have most of my packing already done. Just a few smaller things that wouldn't take no time at all to put together.

Just finishing up the very last of what I needed to put into my last suitcase, then headed towards the kitchen where all were gathered. Warm greetings and the smell of just prepared breakfast filled the air. Taking my place at the table; this was a welcome feeling that I would forever remember. Soft conversation and the morning plans were being made. Only just a few more hours and all of this, would only become a memory. Made me feel sad and a little empty inside. Well, no time for feeling sad now as this was to be a pleasant memory. No room for sadness, not now, not today.

With finishing up and helping Aunt Nellie with clean-up and dishes helped me to take my mind off some things, even if just for a bit. Feeling the need to stay busy, in spite of Aunt Nellie's objection to my help.

Gathering up my suitcases; instead of one, I now had two. Lifting them now from the bedroom floor, brought about a smile and even a softer chuckle. Had no idea, that I had acquired enough for another suitcase in just a few months. Though there were treasures, very personal keep sakes tucked away in those cases.

Taking one long last look around, as not to forget anything, a long sigh of sad departure had now taken over my being.

THE RIDE HOME

With having all of my things packed, I guess the time had really come. It sure was nice to have Aunt Nellie, Uncle Harden, Dessa and Ellie to ride with me to the bus station. It would take us about an hour or so before we reached the station.

We all had remained quiet at first. I can imagine they all must have had thoughts too, that had transpired over the last couple of months. The morning was bright and not a cloud in the sky. Thoughts were broken as the conversation began. With laughter and talk of dreams, it made you feel that life did have a purpose for you. Now, no one ever knows what will happen from one day to the next, I guess that's what makes life and keeps it interesting for sure. At this moment, I was glad that whatever its' purpose, I was going to become a part of it.

Upon arriving at the station, more and more people   began to move about. There sure were a lot of people, of all ages, as they appeared eager to get to their destinations. Stepping out of Uncle Harden's truck; felt as if with each step I took, was another step towards a future that for me, held an uncertainty that I was unsure of. Yet, knowing that without taking that step, I would never know what life had in-store for me. Another adventure in life awaits. Am I correct in saying 'adventure', or should I possibly say; maybe 'destiny'?

Uncle Harden and walked with me inside the station, to claim my ticket. Feeling a bit nervous, why should I be nervous? I had done this before, yet I felt almost numb, yet going through the motions, as if it were someone else standing here.

Now, with my ticket in hand, dawning on me that this was really happening to me. It was actually me, going back to where I had come from. Uncle Harden had placed his hand on my shoulder in comfort. He wasn't a man of many words but had a strong yet gentle approach about him. The thought of my father had entered my mind. As he had done this very same thing, on the day that I had left.

Feeling a bit overwhelmed, as this moment would soon be a memory for me. I would have time to look back on it later, though for now just wanted to enjoy every moment with my extended family. The bus was scheduled to arrive soon, and I didn't want to miss out on any moment that I would have with them.

With all the smiles, the hugs, and stories we told as we waited as patiently, as was possible. The laughter was good as we spoke of what had transpired, feeling like it was just days and not months ago, that I had come to stay with them. Landing my first job as a waitress in this large department store of Kresge's. All the many different things I had learned, which would stay with me, no matter if I used those skills and knowledge somewhere else or just tucked them away in my mind. Deciding either way, it had been a good life experience for me.

Time seemed to move much too quickly as I heard the bus coming up the street. Having so many mixed emotions, I knew what it was, what I needed to do.

We all gathered close, and the warmest felt hugs were being given. I thanked Aunt Nellie and Uncle Harden for their love and for taking me in. For Dessa, she was like a big sister to me, and was there when I needed a big sister to talk to. Ellie gave me the biggest of hugs and told me that I had better write her once, when I arrived home. Ellie, whispering in my ear and asking me if I, had it? I nodded and smiled and promised I would write her. Putting on a sheepish grin behind the warmth that was filling my eyes. It sure felt like I was awfully emotional these last few months. It is what it is, I guess.

The bus had rolled up and the people were starting to make their way, as the line grew a bit longer. Knowing I had to make my way in line and yet also wanting to hold back as long as I could. Aunt Nellie, Uncle Harden, Dessa, and also Ellie, stood as close as they could and would continue to stay; up until I was on board the bus and had found my seat.

Once, I got settled into my seat, making sure and was lucky enough to have gotten a window seat. Looking out now of the window to find the friendly faces that I knew I would miss. Seeing those faces and the love that was behind their eyes, I knew what I was already missing.

Waving good-bye to them as the bus began pulling way. Thinking, now another journey begins. With my head resting on the back of the seat, I decided to close my eyes and hope to relax a bit. It would be about three hours before I reached the depot in Ozark.

I must have napped along the way as time had seemed to fly by and now was awakened to the buss slowing down to make its' stop. Well, am finally here, back in my home state of Arkansas. Now, a new journey and a new chapter begins. Arriving at the depot, everyone on the bus began gathering up their belongings and waited for the moment to begin exiting the bus. For me, I decided to just hang back and stay in my seat. My time for exiting would come soon enough. I didn't have much to gather, just one small bag that I had carried onto the bus. My suitcases were safely tucked away in the storage compartment of the bus. I would be given those once I was safely off the bus.

People were now into the aisle of the bus, standing behind each other so tightly, not giving much way for any other movement. Glad I was still sitting and waiting my turn patiently. Didn't want to feel like a packed sardine in a can. As I waited, I was looking out the small window of where I sat, trying to see if there were any familiar faces waiting to greet me, when I was ready to exit. There were many people waiting for the ones that rode with me here on this bus, and others waiting patiently to come aboard, once the bus was empty. Yet, I searched all the faces, and no one became familiar. Was there no one here to meet me? Had they forgotten that I was to arrive today? Oh my; "Don't start thinking that way", I was telling myself.

Someone was sure to come, right? They would not forget me or not want me back. They knew I was coming home today. The emotions that started to take over, began filling my heart and soul with such sadness, I wasn't really sure anymore of what I should be thinking.

Most everyone was collected by their loved ones and the depot was becoming more and more empty. All the ones that were waiting to enter the door of the bus, were nearly all on. And then, here I was, still waiting. I sure, didn't know what to expect, yet I can't believe that this is what was waiting for me. There was no one here, to greet me, a loved one to collect me and bring me home.

Having made my exit off the bus, I had continued to look around and yet could see no one that was even slightly familiar to me. No one to greet me and welcome me home.

With only a few people left, I found a bench close to a big, shaded tree, only a short distance from all the hustle and bustle of just a few moments ago. Decided, that I might as well rest here and gather the thoughts of what I thought should happen next. My heart felt so heavy, probably much heavier than my two suitcases that were propped up by my side.

As I sat here on this old wooden bench, it was covered by the shade of the leaves of the big old oak. In a sense, it was odd how this old oak, almost felt comforting. To have something strong behind me when the rest of me felt weak.

Gazing up to look at the many shaped clouds that laid peacefully against this blue hue of the sky, it sometimes amazed me how something could be so peaceful, when your inner self was in such heartache. I could not help but wonder; why there was no one here to greet me when I arrived. Closing my eyes to feel the warm breeze as it touched my face, there were tears that had escaped from my eyes. Didn't feel like issuing them away, just chose to just let them fall. Letting my mind wander, how could there be no one. Didn't they know I was coming in on the bus today? Did something happen, and if so, there would be no way of my knowing. Had they not cared, and decided just to leave me here, and I was now on my own. How long would I be here for, before someone would begin to wonder about my presence here, or would they even wonder at all? My heart was breaking into a thousand pieces and I had no one to share my sadness with. Why was I even here? Does anyone hear the sound of my heart as it breaks, breaking like a delicate piece of china? My body was in this place, yet my mind was in another place. Just praying and wishing that things in this young life of mine would be different; a better different. I had cried so many tears, these last few months. Some were from a very sad and lonely heart. As the others had fallen with the thoughts of just wanting to feel wanted and loved. Had no way of knowing what lay ahead for this young life of mine. It was easier for others to say, 'stay positive, things will work out'.

Though to actually be the one it was happening to, was a bit more difficult. I definitely did not think that I would once again, be filled with so much sadness, so soon. With my thoughts in what seemed like a thousand different directions: I was brought back to the happenings of the present. Hearing a car or maybe a truck only a short distance away, I looked up. Was this person or persons, maybe here for me? It was a car and was getting closer and my hopes became more intent. Watching every move this car made, so as not to miss a single movement, I watched as the car found a place to park near the depot building. As I watched intensely, there were two women that had slowly stepped out into the gravel laid parking lot. These two women were searching for someone as their glances viewed the area.

My eyes began to focus a bit clearer now, and I could see them beginning to slowly walk about. Could these two young women be who I thought they were. Oh! My it really was, and I became over filled with such happiness. Was this really happening? These two women were here for me, as they had seen me sitting on this wooden bench, under this big oak tree. Being in such a hurry, I grabbed up my two suitcases and began running towards them. Making certain in my excitement that I wouldn't trip and fall. Feeling very light now on my feet as I grew closer to them. My heart felt like it would have a renewed strength and I would begin to feel whole once more. These two lovely women were my older sisters, that I had not seen in possibly a year or maybe more. A little bit older of course, though here they were. They were here for me. That did not matter right now, because they were here; here for me.

With tightly held hugs, I almost didn't dare to let them go. Having so many questions for them, didn't hardly know where to begin. They reassured me, that we would have plenty of time to catch up and that I would know all that I needed to know. They were just as happy to see me, as I was to see them. It had felt like such a long time since I had even the opportunity to really talk to them. As I would soon have my chance.

Now, my sisters Molly and Madison were very dear to me. They were several years older than myself. So many times, they took care of me, even as an infant. Looking out for me in good times and then also, the not so good times, when they were able.

Our ride home would take some time, so we had plenty of time to talk and catch up on things. Couldn't help to tell them how I felt no one was coming for me. Feeling so alone and had to wonder why there was no one there for me when I had gotten off the bus.

They had told me, that they had gotten a later start than they had wanted. Papa couldn't leave our mother by herself, as she was not feeling well these past few days.

My sisters had only arrived in the early hours before and offered to come and pick me up at the station. If Papa were to need anything while they were gone, there was a neighbor close by if she was needed to help out with my mother. I was rest assured that even with my return, my sisters would be staying on, for at least a week or so.

They wouldn't leave until they knew our mother was better. I was so very glad that they were here and that we could really spend some time together.

I wasn't sure of how much they knew. With my being gone a few months to Aunt Nellie's and Uncle Harden's, I wasn't made aware of my mother not feeling well. I had not received a letter or Aunt Nellie hadn't said anything either. I remember once they had received a letter from Pa, though they hadn't said much about what was in the letter. Had only mentioned a few things, though nothing about my mother being ill. My sisters did mention to me, on our ride home that mother was feeling a bit better and didn't think it was too serious.

Maybe, for my mother to just to rest now a few more days. Our neighbor, the friendly lady that lived just down the road, would come, and stay with mother, when Pa would have to be out in the fields for the day.

We, my sisters, and I, talked of so many things. They had asked me how my stay was at Aunt Nellie's and Uncle Harden's. It was wonderful I told them. They all were so very good to me and had treated me like one of their own family. I excitedly told them about my job at the Kresge's store. It was a really good experience for me. I came to know and understand some people. Of how, busy their lives were. All the hustle and bustle of a much bigger town and so many different places, for people to be.

I had a wonderful time these past few months. Not fully understanding why I was sent away from home, in the first place. Maybe, I'll never really understand it completely. Molly and Madison didn't speak too much of that, only each giving me a weak smile and touched my arm as if they understood. So, I began to realize that they too knew something, yet were not ready to tell me of everything that they knew.

Maybe, whatever they knew, was the reason they were extra loving to me, and even protecting me when they could. Or maybe, it was just because.

Their lives were quite busy too now. My oldest sister, Molly had been married since I was about three years old. She had built a life of her own, with her husband and two small children. They hadn't accompanied her on this trip but were in touch often. Madison was not married, though had come home to help with mother also. They both would stay awhile before heading back to their own homes and their own lives.

We were to arrive soon at the homestead, where Pa would be waiting for us. For me, I was a bit nervous as silly as that may sound. Though I shouldn't be because this was my home. Yet, with my being gone for a few months, I am sure there were changes and not real sure of the kind of welcome I would receive. Though I really shouldn't think this way, it was all that I knew except for the short few months that I was away. I was still nervous and not really sure what to expect, but those feelings of uncertainty, those thoughts needed to be driven and put way back to where I could forget about them, at least one could hope, couldn't they? I tried to be enthusiastic and wanted to make the best of whatever may lie ahead.

HOME

Coming into the drive, I could see not a lot had changed. Pa was out in the fields already, so I would impatiently wait to see him when he came in from the fields. Awaiting anxiously that I would see him later. We were greeted as we made our way to the front porch. The neighbor from just down the road had come to stay with mother for a while, and she greeted us warmly as she was watching our approach as we turned into the drive.

Looking in on mother as she lay resting and choosing not to disturb her, I would again look in on her later. She looked peaceful, resting atop of her feather-filled mattress. Covered with the handmade quilt, I remember helping her with. This was a pleasant memory that I did have with her. Forgetting for a moment, of all the differences we had once encountered.

Being back in the kitchen, there was the smell of freshly baked muffins and the hot water whistling in the kettle for tea. My mother's neighbor was a heavier set woman with grey hair and her face was gentle, yet with the look of a hard life that had set in amongst her features. She was a kind woman, who in the past had helped many neighbors. Being a widow, she enjoyed helping out her friends and neighbors when they needed her. It was good to have her there, keeping mother company.

Carrying my suitcases back to my room, I looked over this room that I had once occupied. Not much had changed in here, everything still seemed the same. I would unpack my things later and went back to where my sisters and Mrs. Flora were, in the kitchen. Settling in at a place at the table where the muffins had been placed and the kettle for tea was ready.

The conversation began with Mrs. Flora, giving us an update on mother. She had been stricken with what the local doctor had called a touch of an infection, or virus. This was a few weeks back and mother still was not her usual self. Though she was feeling better with the worst of it, already passed. She was still too weak to stand for a long period of time. Causing her to be dizzy and unbalanced. She would only eat a little, saying she still wasn't very hungry. So, she rested most of the day, only to come out to sit in her rocker for short periods of time and then back to her bed she would go. I thought it would be nice if I went to see how she was doing, and if she were awake, to ask her if she would like some tea and maybe a muffin. Her room was mostly dark, only a very little light coming in through the thin curtains that hung on the window. Being as quiet as I possibly could, I very softly called out her name. She only stirred but made no sound. Walking back out and gently closing her door, just leaving it open enough to hear her, if she would happen to call out.

Making my way back to the kitchen, my father was now coming in the back screened door. Looking tired from being out in the field most of the morning, he managed a warm hello and a 'welcome home'. With most everyone around the table, Pa slid himself into an open chair. Molly had warmed him up some dinner and I prepared him, his tea. We all talked a while and Pa went quietly to look in on mother, after he had finished with his dinner. She was still resting, and he chose not to want to disturb her.

Our conversation went well into the late of the afternoon. It was nearly time for taking care of the outdoor animals. Pa was about to get up from the table when I offered to go. Telling Pa, that I was happy to be back home, and I am here to help. Telling Pa, to rest, went in to change out of my dress and into more suitable work clothes. The three of them looked at each other and smiled and Pa gave me a smile and got up to give me a hug before I darted off to change. Pa told me, he did miss me and was glad that I was home, and we would talk more later. He wanted to hear all about my time away at Aunt Nellie's and Uncle Harden's.

Now, being already changed, I headed for the barn to take care of the animals that I hadn't seen in a few months. Arriving inside the barn, lay

Chester (the family dog) and my dear companion. He recognized me right off and boy, what an amazingly nice greeting I got. He sure was excited to see me, and I can't tell you, just how an animal can make a person feel being wanted and loved.

Having the animals fed and bedded down for the night, I made my way back towards the house.

The kitchen smelled of freshly baked pies and bread. A smell a person never forgets. My sisters were in the kitchen preparing supper for all of us. Though Pa, was nowhere to be seen. He, as it was mentioned, Pa was in by my mother, so I stayed where I was, as not to disturb them. Offering to help my sisters Molly and Madison, though they didn't need my help. Retiring to my room to unpack everything and to have that off my list. Unpacking wasn't so bad. Looking at all the different things and even a few new pieces of clothing, that I had saved up for. A few small little trinkets: one for my mother and even one for Pa. Hoping that they would enjoy the little pieces that I had purchased for them while I was away. Then, coming across the hand-written note I had gotten from Ellie, the one with this man's name and address on it. This I knew I needed to put in a safe place, a place that only I would remember. Still not sure when I would write him, though the more time that passed, I was certain that I would someday soon, write him a letter. With being satisfied that all my things were unpacked and put away; headed back to where the conversation was in the kitchen. A little louder than what would be considered normal. Though maybe I was wrong about what I was over hearing.

Stepping into the room, the conversations ended, and the room fell silent. Oh! My, what did I walk into? What was it that made everyone fall silent? My eyes traveled across the room and I became aware of my mother. She was sitting in her rocker. The rocker I remembered seeing her in; only days before I had left. Pa and my sisters gave me a week smile, as they looked at me, and then towards my mother. She was now in her favorite rocker, a handmade quilt covering her lap. It was a fall quilt and stitched with love, I had remembered this quilt, it was one of mother's favorites. I remember her working on this from time to time. The things that a person remembers and what it was like. Oh, this I do remember. Feeling just a bit uneasy as to my mother's reaction when she would realize that I was there. Walking softly as I approached her and bending down so that she could see my face; I greeted her with a warm hello. Telling her that I did miss her while I was away and that I was glad to be back. Asking her if she was warm enough and if I could bring her some tea? My mother had always enjoyed a cup of hot tea, even on the warm days that we would get. With the weather cooling off just a bit, she nodded her head yes and I thought just maybe I might have seen a very weak smile on her tired and aging face. Telling her that I would be right back with her tea, I left for the kitchen to prepare her, her tea. Was this a step in the direction of rekindling a relationship with my mother. Don't really know, though I would try and do my best and see where even these small steps would lead. Though, for now I would just accept things as they currently were and just hope and pray that someday they would get better.

Bringing my mother her tea, she reached out for it and accepted it. Didn't say a word or meet my eyes, though for now, at least she knew I was standing there and had graciously taken the tea that was made.

DON'T REMEMBER

In the days that followed, it seemed as though my mother was beginning to gain a bit more of her strength. She would come out of her room more often and began eating somewhat more than what she had before. Seeing her also, sit in her favorite rocker and hearing the creak in the floor as it kept time like a pendulum clock. These were more like the days that I remembered.

As she began to move more and more about our home, my sisters were making plans on heading back to their own homes. It would happen by the end of the following week. Being carefully certain that mother was getting back to her old self, or at least to the way she was before this infection had taken ahold of her.

I sure was going to miss them, (my sisters) when it came time for them to leave. It had been really nice having them here. Yet, I knew they were feeling somewhat anxious to get back to where they were needed too. So many things, so many changes. It hardly felt real, yet it was very real. Even if I wasn't sure how to take it all in just now. Time and events always seem to keep moving forward. Accepting it, definitely was a life building block for me. And to just think of it, I had thought about school, yet feeling saddened that I would no longer be able to go. Hadn't thought much about that lately. Being so preoccupied over the summer months, with being away at Aunt and Uncle's, and with mother and having my sisters' home. Hadn't had thought much of school lately and how I would miss going. Though, I did miss by best friend 'Frankie'. We had been best friends, for as long as I can remember. She was one of the best. Feeling I should try and see her, before my sisters leave. Then I wouldn't have to worry too much about mother, if I were away for an afternoon. Thinking more about her now, I really did miss her. With thoughts of Frankie, now filling my mind and how we use to spend as much time together as we could. Knowing I needed to make those plans soon before time slipped away on me.

As we all had sat down to supper one cool evening, it was my mother who felt strong enough to join us. It had brought back so many memories with all of us at the same table. Glancing around at each of them, my eyes became focused on my mother. As she too, was glancing around the table at all of us when her eyes stopped as she looked at me or was it maybe even a glare. It was as if she was looking right through me. My hand had gripped my glass so tight, I felt that it might break beneath my fingers. As she started speaking to me, it was as if she wasn't really seeing me. What a horrible feeling. My mother's words were to me, "I Don't Remember You", "Who Are You"? My heart just sank like I was being drowned in quicksand. Everyone had stopped anything and everything that they had been doing or saying. I think they may have been more startled by this comment, than me. As I looked at her; I said, "Mom, it's me; Sarah, you remember me, right?

She just looked at me as you could see her mind trying to remember. As she spoke, she said "You were a mistake and if you had to be born, you should have been born a boy". I said, "Why would you say that"? As she turned her eyes away from me, she said "A boy". I don't think anyone was more hurt, than me. The others just looked at her and didn't know what to say. Those words felt sharp, it was like a cold bladed knife had just stabbed me in the heart. I could hardly believe the words that I had just heard. For such a long, long time, I had always felt that way, and now those thoughts that I had felt so many months before, were actually true. Was it really my mother, who had just spoken those words, words you could never take back? And yet, with what I was feeling, how could that compare to actually hearing them. No one could speak just then, and we all looked at each other for an answer. Though there just did not seem to be one. My mother removed herself from the table and walked slowly to sit in her favorite rocker. Not even excusing herself, just walked away. With not any one of us being able to speak, it was just as if time had just stood still.

GETTING AWAY

Feeling the urgent need to rush from the table, that we just all were gathered at, and at the same time while trying to hide the warm sensation that began to swell in my eyes, with trembling words I spoke, telling my father and my sisters that I needed a bit of time. It was like not being able to move from the spot that held me there. My feet feeling like anchors, yet my heart and soul felt like it was just tossed away, tossed away into a sea of hurtful things. With not much now left of an appetite, that hunger had disappeared. Struggling now to pull my feet from the anchors that held them to the floor. I excused myself and stepped outside where the air was cool. A feeling of being suffocated by emotion, I had the feeling and the need for fresh and cooler air.

Moving now as quickly as my feet would carry me, I went towards the door, and slowly stepped outside. As I looked out into the evening sky, there were many stars out tonight and the moon nearly full. It was a calm night, with just a warm and gentle breeze. Wondering to myself now, how could there be such a beautiful night, when I felt like I didn't even know who I was or even where I was supposed to belong. Oh, how I just wanted to run away from all of this, yet my feet weren't moving anymore. Just standing motionless now in this moment, taking in the night air.

My mind began to replay the moments that had led up to my being where I am right now. It felt more like a nightmare than just a hurtful memory. How could those moments have gone so wrong? This was my mother, a mother whom I had thought loved me, even though she had never uttered those words to me. I didn't think that she had treated me so awfully bad. Just never showed me that she appreciated me. I had thought that she or it, was just the way that it was. No, I think I am just kidding myself in thinking those things. I had seen other families show even just a little bit of love and or appreciation of one another. I knew this from watching them, that this was something I had wished I had, but didn't. Feeling like my mind now was in such a fog, the tears that I tried so hard to hold back, were now streaming down my now tired face, flowing uncontrollably. Taking in deep breaths of air, hoping that I could somehow control the bitterness and hurt I was feeling. Wanted to scream, scream so loud to let the hurt out. Even the mountains, way off in the distance, would echo that most mournful cry back to me. Thoughts of 'I can't believe this was happening to me, kept repeating itself, over and over again. What did I do? Where did I go wrong? Was I really that bad of a person, or for that matter, a daughter? Had I felt this before, but just ignored it? I wasn't sure of any of that anymore. Couldn't make any sense of any part of it.

I had no idea of how long I had been standing outside in the night air. Began feeling that no matter how long I had been out there, I had made a promise to help out with the supper dishes and, yet I was still out here. Even though my world, as I knew it; had just been shattered. It was still important for me to keep my promise. I would face whatever was in store for me once I stepped back inside. Feeling a bit sick now to my stomach of having to face everyone, including my mother. A mother who hadn't wanted me in the first place. I made my way ever so slowly back inside to the home, I thought I knew and to the people inside that were my family.

Stepping inside now, the conversations that were spoken were now a bit on the quieter side. My mother was still in her rocking chair, slowly rocking back and forth, and it was keeping time, just like that pendulum clock that lay a top of the fireplace mantel. I wanted to talk to her, but the words wouldn't come and feeling frozen to the spot where I stood. Softly, I made a few steps towards her and gently called out her name. She stopped rocking, looked at me and then looked away. She began again in the constant pattern of her rocking. Just standing there, I didn't know if I should cry, scream at her or run away from her. So many feelings, so many emotions raining down on me, I wasn't sure of what to do or say next. Then I felt some one's hand on my shoulder, in a comforting sort of way. As, I slowly closed my eyes, the tears that I was holding back, had only found a way to escape once again. Now, opening my eyes and turning ever so slightly, it was my father standing right behind me. It was his hand on my shoulder. I looked up at him, with pleading eyes and he gestured for me to follow him. As I followed him through the dim lit kitchen and then outside to our front porch, we each took a seat on the top step.

It was my father who had spoken first. In his best comforting tone, he was trying to assure me, that everything that was happening to my mother, was not my fault and to not be so hard on myself. I know he tried to sound convincing, but it wasn't making my heart feel any better. I asked him questions, trying to find some answers that would somehow satisfy this deep sadness that had overtaken my being. I felt love from my father as we sat there together, just he and I talking. Even though he wasn't a man of free expression, he was doing well by me, in his soft-spoken words and his understanding of the brokenness that I felt.

Not, exactly sure just how long Pa and I sat there, though we knew it had to be getting a bit late. As my father stood, he was helping me to my feet, and we walked inside together. My sisters, Molly and Madison softly greeted us as we came in, being careful not to let the screen door close with a bang behind us. They had hot tea ready for us and it sure was a welcomed sight. It seemed to be a comfort as I held the warm almost hot cup, wrapping my fingers around it.

Mother was nowhere in sight. Thinking that she had gone off to her room for the night. My sisters had confirmed my thoughts and that she hadn't said much before retiring to her room. Father went in to check on her and was gone for a little while. It was Molly and Madison and myself at the table and we spoke in soft conversation. They had observed the hurt that remained in my eyes and the sadness that still seemed to overtake my face, not to say the sadness that my heart felt. They were not sure of what to say to me, yet their words of comfort did lighten the ache in my heart, some. Saying to me; that no matter the words that our mother had spoken, whether she meant them or not, they would not have it any other way that I was and would always be their little sister. That they loved me beyond words. Telling me, that they weren't exactly sure where those words had come from that my mother had spoken. Only thinking, that maybe it was because our mother had lost a child and inwardly wanting her next child to be a boy. Not saying that, that was an excuse for my mother's words, but could have had a bit of a factor in her actions tonight. The young girl that would have been my older sister, was only 3 years old when she died. Now only pictures and memories remained of her. Well, that is all I would have of her is the pictures. I knew and I understood sadness and what it felt like to feel empty. Now, I won't make excuses for my mother, though maybe her grief after all this time was greater than anyone knew. Even though my heart was broken, I would still try and love the mother that I wanted her to be. Was this right? I don't know. For as long as I had to or was living here, I would do my best to try and do what was right by her and love her, even though she would not let it be easy. I'm sure there would be days, when I would be the one feeling like, would it be worth my trying, only to have those hurtful feelings resurface themselves. Yes, I had to, needed to keep trying to reach the mother that I once remembered.

DAWN OF A NEW DAY

It has been said that things will always look better or brighter in the morning. I guess you could believe it if you wanted to. There are many times where this way of thinking does actually make a lot of sense, many situations have proven this way of thought. Though, for me I'm not sure exactly how I felt, yet needed to focus on other things as well.

Still feeling pretty numb about the previous day and the nights' events and have decided that today was going to be a better day. Knowing I only had a couple of weeks left before school would start for Frankie. I made plans to go and see my best friend. Had so much to tell her, and I really did miss her. We used to spend lots of time together, yet now it was life's events that were keeping us apart. Not today, I told myself. I would be sure that my chores were complete, and my sisters were still here to help with my mother. Getting the okay from my father and my sisters, I would leave for Frankie's just after lunch. Mother hadn't hardly spoken to me all morning, let alone make any eye contact with me. That made moving about our home, very uncomfortable, but what was I to do? What would it be like, when my sisters finally went back home, and I would be here alone with my mother? Was I afraid of her? There's no use in fretting over it, things would soon change and there was no stopping that.

It was just shortly after lunch, and helping with clean up, I was getting ready to visit Frankie. Only moments before heading out the door, my mother asked if I was leaving; turning to look at her, I greeted her in a very polite way, and told her I was going to visit Frankie and would be back before dark. She didn't say anything, just looked at me. My father and sisters wished me a nice visit with Frankie and told them I would be back before dark. All I had gotten from my mother was a blank stare. Not to hesitate any longer, and out the door I went.

Walking along our long driveway to the road was in its' own way, relaxing. The sun was out, yet not real hot today. The tall trees alongside the driveway were casting their own shadows. Gentle breezes filled the air and it felt good to see all that was around me. This was taking my mind off of things, that I didn't want to think about just now. The walk to Frankie's would take a while. She lived about 3 miles from me. The walk would do me good.

Arriving at Frankie's, she was just as excited as I was, when we saw each other. She was keeping herself busy with her own chores outside when I arrived. What a welcome site she was. I really did miss this girlfriend of mine. We sat together for what seemed like hours. Had so many things to catch up on. I listened very intensely as she spoke of adventures and of the several weeks that I had been away. Then, I in turn caught her up on all that had been happening to me. Seemed, as if there wasn't enough time in a day for us to share all that we had wanted.

It was getting to be extremely late in the afternoon when I had to leave for home and started out for my journey back. Now, with the sun casting shadows behind me and the day had started to cool down, I would still make it home in time to help with chores. Yes, indeed it was a visit to remember. Frankie will always be my absolute best friend, no matter where our paths in life would take us. We had renewed our pact that day and now once again, we will be bound as eternal friends.

A NEW BEGINNING

As the hours turned into days, it was only a matter of time now, for when my sisters would be leaving. Wasn't sure just how I felt, yet I knew of what had to be. My being alone with my mother was causing some relentless anguish. I know it almost felt foolish to me yet couldn't ignore the annoying ache in the pit of my stomach. After all, she was my mother, why should I be afraid of her? Maybe, it wasn't so much as being afraid of her, as it was not knowing exactly how to cope with the way she was acting towards me. It always made me so uneasy, though I would do my best in being polite and respectful towards her. Father didn't say too much, though he did offer words of comfort when she would go a little too far. This is what I had to look forward too? Not real excited about that. Decided that with whatever happened or would happen, I would search for that inner strength, the strength that somehow pushed people into not giving up. I knew it was there, just needed, for it to surface when I would need it most.

The days had come, and the days had passed. My sister's Molly and Madison had already left, promising to keep in touch. Now, it was my mother, my father and me, here at home to get back to what was supposed to be considered normal. Mother hadn't changed a whole lot in the days that had come and gone.

School had already started for the year, yet I no longer would be attending our small school. I chose to replay the memories that I had, when Frankie and I had become friends and now we were the very best of friends. With everything that had happened over the course of the past few months, I was needed at home now to help. My mother, she was a bit better in the way that she could move around a bit more, yet still needed assistance with quite a few other things and that is where I came in.

It was an early evening in the early days of December, when the thought of this man had come into my mind once more. Mother had gone to her room and father sat in his favorite chair. Pulling out his pipe and tobacco and it was him this time that I noticed how his mind had drifted off to another place. Wondering where it was, that he had taken his mind and where it had drifted off to. It may have been like a ship on the ocean, just drifting with no set course in mind or possibly a destination that was only known to the captain of this vessel. Wasn't for certain, of the kind of relationship he had with my mother, yet I felt there had to be something there, that was only known to them. It was their bond and I only being considered a child, did not yet know of such a relationship. Yet, there was something strong between them and it was one thing I could hold on to. My father wasn't leaving her in her time of need.

Sitting now at the table with no one to interrupt me, I decided to write this man a letter. This man's name was Sam. Thoughts had flooded my mind, where would I begin or what would I even say? Had made myself a cup of hot tea and made one for father as well. As he reached for it and took it from my hand, he gave me a smile without words. Smiling back, I had said to him, "I love you Papa. "Thank you for loving me back." These words were almost a whisper. He gently touched my hand and then drifted off once more, into the world where he had been only just moments ago.

Getting back to this letter now. I began to put together a letter for this man whom I only knew of his name.

Surprising myself, the words were actually not that hard to come by, as I began writing. The thoughts flowed to paper as if they were meant to be there. Grabbing myself one more cup of hot tea, I continued to write. As it was getting to be more into the hours of the night, I chose to finish this letter. Needing to be sure to walk it to the mailbox in the early morning. I wasn't sure just when he would receive it, and I would wait patiently. for a return letter. My mind rested a bit easier now, as I tidied up a bit before taking myself off to bed. Morning would come early and needed to get an early start on the list that seemed to be endless of the things that I wanted to be able to accomplish. Things would get better; I was sure of it. It was important for me to stay optimistic, though it wasn't going to be easy.

As the days passed one into the other seeming as if they flowed much too close together. The letter seemed like it was all that kept me going. I tried to occupy my days with what time I had, to do and what I needed to be doing for my mother and also, for my father. It seemed rather strange somehow, that with Frankie and the other kids all in school, it felt like I was missing out on being with my friends and the learning that I could be doing, maybe somehow, it was actually a blessing in disguise, not sure how just yet, but maybe if it were, it would show itself to me someday soon.

I had plenty done by the time mother started to move about. As she entered the room, I tried to be cheerful and welcoming her, only to be greeted by a most heavy sigh. I tried not to show the hurt that I felt and smiled weakly, in offering her some breakfast and tea. Motioning to me with just a wave of her hand, I continued to prepare a dish for her just in case she would eat, even just a bit. Carrying on a conversation was not at all successful, as she wouldn't respond to anything that I would say. How dis-heartening this all was and yet, I struggled to keep going what nearly felt like almost every day.

So many days were like this one, always seeming to be so uncertain and creating such an uneasy feeling in the lowest pits of my stomach. Why should I, or anyone for that matter; or how do people work this out, for it all to disappear? Then, my mind would tell me "it will get better, don't lose faith". As hard as it is and how broken I felt, I would do my very best to beat this feeling of defeat. It's not happening today or any day for that matter, that feeling of defeat would not have me as its' prize. Not as long as, I have faith on my side, and I knew that faith was much stronger than defeat.

So, if I said it before, I would say it again, and again, however many times it takes. My time, my days they may be numbered, though I know there will be a time when I can honestly say: This is

going to be the day of NEW
BEGINNINGS for me.

LOVE GROWS

Feels like so much time has passed, and Lord knows there has been so many things that have happened, how does a person recall all those moments and recapture its' happenings? A person just does, I guess each in their own way, whatever that may be. Whether in your mind as a memory or something that you had decided to write down for future reference. This is something that I had done. Writing to this man who lived so many miles from me. You ask your self-questions, yet I don't get too carried away with trying to answer them all. You see, some of those questions are not meant to have an answer, at least not in the timing that you thought you should have them. They will be answered in their own time.

Receiving letters from this man; this man's name is Sam who, when I received his first written letter back to me, my fingers trembled with excitement as I fumbled and being so extra careful in the opening of his letter. Reading his letter and then re-read it again. Now, just looking at these pages that were held by my nervous fingers, I knew that I needed to get another letter off to him as soon as I possibly could. Feeling that this would be the start of a new-found friendship in an un-seen face. All the feelings of uncertainty that I had once felt, no longer existed. I had found a new friend, even if it was just in letters for now.

It had only been just a couple of days and I had another letter from Sam. Wondering of course, what did Sam think of my letters to him? With whatever he was thinking and whatever he may have been doing after the war, I was sure when he was ready, he would share that with me too someday. Though in the meantime, we would have our letters that we would share our thoughts, our dreams, and our ideas, with each other.

Trying to stay occupied and keeping quite busy with helping my mother as she was getting around much better, yet her words were still very few to me and not for any real conversations with me. I don't know if I will or would ever get use to things being this way. Yet, I was learning a lot from her even before she had taken ill. Now, it was just doing most of those things by myself and continued learning and trying to understand all that I could.

Time was moving forward into the weeks ahead and very important decisions needed to be made. Some days were just okay, others at times were the most terrible of days. Not too many were good days. Just mustering through and trying to make the best of a very uncomfortable situation. Even though I felt like I didn't belong, this was still my home. I longed for the letters that I received from Sam, and as soon as I could, I would write him back. His letters took me to a place that only he and I shared. I looked forward to his letters, as with this, I felt that this is what helped in keeping me going each day. Or at least this was a big part of that. This was our time.

My days of attending school had been cut short. With which I had mentioned before. I was needed more at home to help with my mother and be of whatever help I could be, to my father. Working the fields with him and tending to the animals was just the start. I only knew the basics of math and though my spelling was quite strong for a person my age, going further on with school would just have to wait.

It was now winter, and it was settling in with full force. The winds were awfully ferocious, creating drifts in the most of unusual places. It had been good to have gotten an early start on the wood. As to see the looks of things, we were going to need plenty of it. Bringing in an abundance of wood so that the fireplace and even the cook stove (sometimes used as heat) would not go out in the middle of the night. This along with all of my other chores were very endless, or that is the way it seemed most days. There was always an awful lot to do.

Sometimes, I thought it was more than what I was capable of, yet I still managed and got through it.

Unknowingly it was making me stronger.

Winter seemed long and unusually cold for being the middle of January. Though, I guess we did get through it, just like a lot of our neighbors did. Always ready when possible to help our neighbors as they would do the same for us in a time of need.

Have been receiving letters from Sam on a pretty regular basis now. It always lightened my heart when his letters came. They gave me a new and brighter insight to this new-found friendship that I have found with him. So, as soon as time would allow, I would sit sometimes by the light of the oil lamps and write him a letter in return. With this and along with the fire that was already burning in the fireplace, it would give off its' generated heat that would fill the room. It was more than a welcome, to feel the heat on a cold winter's night.

Pa was in his rocker reading the daily newspaper and my mother just sat rocking in her chair. The two of them rocking was in unison. It was like creek, creek and then crack, crack. Almost funny the way they seemed to keep time just opposite of each other. Before long, my mother was on her way to her room, moving or maybe gliding across the floor. I wished her a good-night and asked her if there was anything that I could get for her. She turned to look at me, though first at Pa, shook her head and then continued onward to her room. Pa then looked at me, half smiled and nodded his head at me, then went back to reading his paper.

Never was quite sure if they knew who it was that I was writing letters to, but that didn't matter right now. If I needed to explain it later, then I would. Though for now, this was my time and enjoyed writing this new-found friend of mine.

Pa could see a change in me, yet he didn't ask me about it. Maybe he wasn't sure he if he should, but if he did know something, he wasn't mentioning it. He didn't treat me or talk to me differently, at least not in a harsh way. Pa and I continued to work together outside, and I was still helping my mother with what I could do inside. The days and nights seemed to pass rather quickly, and I guess I was in a way grateful for that. My mother's conversation was a bit more these days, though only to my father. She did speak to me, though more like a hired hand than a daughter. It's just not the relationship that I had always thought a mother-daughter. relationship would be like. Right then, I knew that if ever someday I would have children, I did not want it to be like my mother was with me. Even if affection wasn't something that was displayed in public, I would show my children love and talk to them in the way my mother couldn't or wouldn't show it to me. Who knows what the future holds for any one of us? Though, I knew my someday would come, just didn't know when. Yet, I will welcome it also not to forget where it was, I had come from.

It had been a few weeks when I felt so pre-occupied in doing and carrying out my responsibilities of going through the motions in trying to keep my family's home together, when it was a day in February that I had received a letter from Sam. I had received a Christmas card from Sam back then, and yet this one seemed to be a bit thicker than his previous letters. With my nervousness, it was making my fingers tremble just a bit. I headed out towards the field and sat down on a huge rock that nestled beside the big maple. The sun was out and not too cold today for a day in February yet feeling the crispness of the air seemed to bring about a newness that I never had felt before. I had become extremely focused as to what this letter from Sam would contain, I slowly began to read his letter. Sam's friendship and mine had grown over these last months and it had begun to be something incredibly special between us. Something that was his and mine alone. I would have never thought it possible, but now I think that I was truly mistaken of my thoughts that had consumed me in the past several months. The faith that I knew as a child seemed to resurface and has awakened in my being. Sam 's words I felt, were amazing as I read them and then over again. In this one and incredibly special letter, my Sam was proposing marriage to me. This was so exciting, so special, and so new. In whatever it was that I was feeling, there was nothing bad about any of it. I would write him back yet today with my answer, and with a little bit of money that I still had left from my waitressing days, I would send this return letter express delivery. I wanted him to receive my response as quickly as the post office could deliver.

Some may not understand, yet I knew that there were many that would. Sam, a man I had never met in person, yet having our photos of each other and our very own words we shared, they were ours and only ours. Could this be what was waiting for me all along?

Thank goodness, now with the letter written and mailed, I went back to the tasks at hand. Trying to carry on about my normal routine was not at all easy these next few weeks. If my mother and father had known about my new-found friendship, not at all sure how they would react. My thoughts I guess for now were focused on my father, for he has always given me positive encouragement in whatever I did. Still my mother, was my mother even though it was difficult to relate to her these past few months, yet I still would do my best towards her, still helping in all that I could. Though, I had given and will continue to do so, for her sake, for Papa's and even my own.

ANTICIPATION

The weeks seemed to pass by so quickly, almost like a moving train at high speed. Then on the other hand, almost to the pace of an aging tortoise walking along a deserted highway. In either case, I was waiting for the one letter from Sam, telling me when he would be on his way.

Pa had noticed a change in my behavior over these past few months and did now decide to make ask me about it. I had decided then, that I would be honest with my father. It brought back a lot of memories for me when I started talking to him. My mother had already gone to her room for the night, and I had decided that I would somehow, someday tell her too, of what I had planned or at least that's what my thoughts were. My father looked a bit sad and didn't even get angry. Just said he understood, yet at the same time, didn't want me to leave. My father and I had a very grown-up conversation and it felt good, but a little scary at the same time to tell him of my pending plans. He no longer treated me like a young child, but rather a young woman who had to grow up much faster than her years. This did bring some sadness, for the both of us. I strongly believe that this had brought us closer than we had ever been.

The sun rose early this morning and it felt like it would be an early Spring.

Now whether that would actually be, I don't know, but it sure did feel like it today.

Mother came out of her room just as I was putting hot tea and biscuits on the table. The smell of fresh baked biscuits had filled the air. Looking up at my mother, I offered her to sit and I would gladly get her some tea and a fresh warm biscuit. She just looked at me and made her way to the table. Which at the same time my father was coming in from early morning chores. He commented on how nice the fresh baked smell was that had filled the kitchen and took a seat next to my mother. Saying grace, was something that our family had done for years, as this day shouldn't be any different, yet somehow it felt different. I decided to take the lead on this one. My mother gave me a very strange look, one that a person doesn't forget too easily. I tried hard not to let it bother me the best that I could and began with grace for what we were about to eat.

With cleaning, up the table and dishes done, I thought that maybe I would try and talk to my mother of what I had been so uncertain of in telling her. I tried speaking to her, but she wouldn't even look at me or acknowledge me when I tried speaking her name. I couldn't believe how this was going. In the months now that I have been home, she hardly spoke to me at all. What she would say to me, wasn't worth mentioning, at least not now, or maybe never. I don't know.

Moving about and taking care of the house and then moved outside to help Pa. My mother had gone off to her room and halfway closed the door. Letting her know where I would be in case, she would happen to wonder where Pa and I had gone. She was quiet yet and had nodded her head. Being sure that she was all right, I headed for the outdoors. Pa was busy in the barn and I greeted him and offered to help. Mother was fine and, in her room and told her where you and I would be, just so she knew, is what I had told my father.

Pitching in to help him, I started in, on tending and feeding the animals, then cleaning the barn. Once all was done, I turned the animals out into the pasture. The day itself, was rather nice. The sun was out, and the warmth made you feel good against the coolness of the air that still lingered on this day in February. Pa stayed busy in the barn in which there were a few things that needed fixing. With everything good out here, I went back inside to check on my mother. With it being almost lunch time, I quickly checked in on her, finding that she had fallen asleep.

Heading out to tell Pa, I was going to pick up the mail and when I returned, I would start us some lunch. Mail was delivered to our mailbox, that was at the end of our driveway. We did have a post office which was inside our general store. Very small and quaint, yet it offered all that we needed without having to travel into Ozark. Only traveled into Jethro, on certain days that I would need to visit our local general store. In traveling that road on occasion, it was a very winding road, some would say it was as crooked as a dog's hind leg. Finding then that if I would leave earlier in the morning, then I could be back home just before lunch time. Though today was a day that mail would be delivered to our mailbox down at the end of our driveway. Maybe it was just me today yet chose to walk a bit faster, faster than I would have on days before. With having high hopes that a letter from Sam would be waiting for me there.

Arriving now at the mailbox, there actually was quite a bit of mail today. Quickly scanning the contents that I held in my hand, there were letters to my Mother and also for Pa. Then, there it was, the one I had been waiting so patiently for. It was my letter from Sam. I could hardly wait to read it. Making sure as not to drop any of all the mail I had gathered from the box, I made my way back up to the house.

Putting the bulk of what there was for mail on the kitchen table, I headed towards my room with the letter from Sam. Letting my father know of the mail first, that I had placed on our kitchen table.

Settling in my room, I was eager to read my letter from Sam. Now, I was carefully reading and even re-reading every word. I could hardly believe it, but it was right here in black and white. With over whelming emotions, Sam was planning a trip here, here to see me. His plans and mine, Sam and I were to be married. This was exciting news. For two people who had begun a friendship with our letters to each other, then for this very much valued friendship to develop into a love that was only ours. I don't know of too many people that would or could understand a love like this. Maybe, you had to be in a love of this kind to understand the feelings of two people that it involved. But no matter what, this was a very special day, today with my new love and a new beginning that would start the meaning of (the rest of my life). Now, it felt like there was so much to do and so much to plan for. Not sure exactly when I could begin all this planning, but knew it needed to be soon. It would all work out, my taking a deep breath and taking it all in, I would begin the planning very soon. I don't remember the last time I felt this excited, or I felt this kind of happiness.

Sam 's arrival would come in late March and we would be married then and start our life together. So, I needed to start planning for when Sam would arrive. It would only be a matter of a couple weeks to three before the day came that I would meet this new-found love of my life.

I AM READY

With so much planning to be done, I would wonder just a bit if I would have everything I needed when the time would come, when meeting Sam. There wasn't anyone other than Frankie that I could really talk to, about all of this. Though I did have her address and I made a promise to her that I would send her mine as soon as Sam and I were settled in our own home.

I had tried to talk to my mother, yet it was still difficult but never gave up in trying to reach her. She had her good days, and then of course her not so good days. I never was too sure if I would be able to talk to her, to reach her before I left. With the thought of this, it did make me feel sad. I would have liked to have shared many moments with her, not only this but so many other things with her, but how do you share something with someone, when they don't seem to care if you are there or not. You might think that I should try harder, but you don't know me, the painful memories that I carry, and yet, I still I did not give up. Maybe, someday she would talk to me again, but for now I would not give up in trying to reach her. Whether it be before I leave or even after I have gone. I will always try to reach her, to try and reach her cold and distant heart.

I have decided that when the day arrives, whether it be wrong or right, I would at least leave her a long letter before I go. I know what that may sound like, yet I will not just blurt it out to her. Sometimes for me, writing things down and expressing what it is I feel, is just much easier than just crying it out and hope I don't say something hurtful that I can't take back.

I know that my father would understand, but not my mother. Which I feel is incredibly sad. This is not the kind of relationship that I would have thought, to have with my mother. Well, can't go back and change the past. I only need to hopefully make them better for her, for Papa and for myself. Not sure just how I'll make that happen yet. So, we'll see how the next few days progress.

The upcoming days had kept me quite busy. With an awful lot on my mind and still plenty to do here at home, feeling like I didn't have time to tend to the things that I needed. Though I continued working at what needed to be, and it all eventually came together. In a way it was a good thing, kept my mind off of the things that made me feel sad, so for right now, I really didn't want to dwell on any of the hurt.

Only a couple days to go, I would be starting a very new chapter in my life. Meeting this man, who has captured my heart and soul and soon to become his wife. When you think of it, it may sound a bit scary, but yet intriguing and so new. I am extremely excited about all this, though the anticipation runs hot through my veins as I let my mind wander into the unknown of things. Yet, after all this, I am not afraid only a bit sadden that I leave this life behind and also feeling joyous to enter into a life of hopes and dreams. I know things in life are not always easy and there will be times when my life and my husband to be may be challenged. Yet, this man; Sam he loves me, and I love him. We will take our love and our marriage day by day, and by the grace of God, he will sustain us in all that we need and do. I will pray for my mother and my father whom in which many times, I have called papa. I know that my father is sadden but yet, he understands. My mother still does not acknowledge me, or at most even try and talk to me.

Though I still do love her and yet don't always understand her. I have written her a letter about my departure. Now, you may not understand it now, or you may not understand it at all. But I would ask that you keep an open mind and maybe possibly even an open heart, to understand it, if even just for a little. Tomorrow is the biggest day of my life. So, here is to preparations and willful undertakings. How do I begin this day? Well, I guess one might say at the beginning, right? Let me see if that is where I can begin.

Waking early just at the break of dawn. It already felt like it would be a most beautiful Spring Day. The leaves were already budding on the trees and the grass turning that dark, rich shade of green. I hadn't heard anyone stirring about, so wasn't sure if anyone was yet awake. Decided to start moving about and yet didn't want to wake anyone, being this early in the morning. I know I had plenty to do before leaving for Ozark to meet Sam.

Being what I thought was a nice gesture, I began working on a genuinely nice breakfast for my mother and father. Putting a pan of biscuits in the oven and started frying up some bacon and eggs. Maybe, the smell of this would wake them, I didn't know, yet remained hopeful. Thinking that I wanted them to have a nice breakfast before my father started with his day. My mother, I wasn't sure if she would be willing to eat or not, though it was prepared for her, if she decided. Once this was all complete and still warm and, in the oven, now waiting for them. I began packing up a few things, that I know I would want and needed to take with me. It didn't seem like I had very much, but yet again, I guess how much does a young girl acquire and take with her? Knowing that this would be the last time she would actually call this her home. So many memories, some good and then some not. Didn't want to dwell too much on the past. This was a special and exciting day and didn't want anything to ruin it. Having all three suitcases packed now, concentrated on myself now, getting ready sure made me nervous. Though nervous in a good way. With so many thoughts running

183

through my mind, wasn't sure just how to begin or where to start. It would all fall into place; I was sure that it would.

With the letter already written to my mother and the one that I had written for Pa. He knew what it was that I was doing, and yet, wanted to express to him in a letter how I had felt and thanking him in many ways too. Taking both of the letters and propping them up against the oil lamp that rested in the middle of our kitchen table. A letter to Pa, and one for my Mother. Nearly bringing tears to my eyes once more, I couldn't believe in many ways that I was leaving like this. It wasn't the way that I would have thought that my life events would have gone. But here I am. Life is sure strange sometimes, makes you wonder why and where is it, in life you are headed?

Pa had awakened now and was moving about. Coming into the kitchen, the smell of biscuits and bacon still lingered in the air and were still warm. My father looked at me and had given me a faint smile and thanked me for the breakfast that there was. My father and I we talked a bit and softly as not to awaken my mother. His eyes were sad as he spoke to me. He knew

I was leaving this morning and caught a glimpse of the letters that were addressed to my mother and him, that lay propped on the kitchen table. He didn't say much, only that he understood. We had a very nice conversation, my father and I. These are memories that I would take with me, and no one can take them away. I didn't want to cry, yet felt like I was fighting the tears, not allowing them to run down my cheeks. My voice was cracking a little as he told me he knew, and he understood, yet he would always love me no matter what and to keep in touch always. As I made this promise to my father, he left for the work in the fields. This was to be the last I would see of my father, or at least for some time to come.

As the time drew near, I finished up with a few things and had decided to leave my suitcases by the door of what was my bedroom. Leaving was going to be a bit hard, after all, I grew up here or at least a small portion of my life had been here. Oh, the memories I had and even more memories to make. With one last walk through, I let everything that I saw, work its way into my memory as not to forget the life that I had here. Feeling sadden just a little, it would soon be just that, a memory. Looking in on mother one last time to see if she was awake, which she didn't stir even as I softly called out her name. Had thought it best then, not to disturb her. Taking more than a moment to look at her and really seeing her. Lying there on her feather-filled mattress and covered with the quilt that I had helped her with. That was a nice memory to keep. Yet now things seemed to be, oh! So different. Where had those good memories gone? Well, can't dwell too much on that, just remember what was. Now, slowly closing; just slightly her door so that she wouldn't be disturbed by any outside noises.

I really didn't like leaving, without being able to talk to her. Though, I did try and was not successful. Thoughts of this, made my heart feel heavy. I would write her and Pa later when I got a bit settled in my new life with Sam. This was important to me and this I would do. Feeling the anticipation of only a few moments away, I would be heading out that door and only returning to pick up the few suitcases that I had already packed.

The letters that I had written for my mother and Pa still lay propped where I had left them. This way they would be sure to notice them. One long glance around the home that I knew, and with a sense of sadness that overtook me, as my mind was capturing the memories in this house. Shaking that off, then smiling faintly I walked out the door.

Stepping out onto the porch, being sure that the door didn't bang shut, my eyes searched for my father. Seeing him just a short distance into the field, I knew that he wouldn't be able to hear me, if I were to call out to him. Even though knowing this, I softly called out to Pa and waving at him a gentle good-bye. I Love You papa and I will write. Making my way down our drive to the road, I would catch a ride into town with the mail truck. It was about 10 miles into town, and I knew that he; the mail man, would be alright with me hitching a ride with him into town.

Not real sure of how long I had waited for the mail truck, though I knew it wasn't long and I could hear the sound of the truck off in the distance. He was approaching, and I would be ready. The time was getting ever so close now, for my meeting Sam. It must have been nerves, or maybe even butterflies. I was nervous but excited at the very same time. Before I knew it, that time would be happening very soon. My mind had drifted off just for a bit, and the sound of the mail truck grew much closer. (How does a person check their appearance without a mirror)? Well, I just had to know that I was simply fine and would be a bit more concerned once I reached Ozark.

My future now only lay a short time away. As the mail truck approached and stopped only a short distance from my feet, He greeted a warm hello and asked if I per chance needed a ride? Letting him know that I was headed into Ozark, he offered to give me a lift into town. Passing casual conversation was pleasant, as he didn't ask too many questions. We spoke of simple things and it stayed pleasant. It didn't seem to take long, this journey of mine into town. Thanking my driver, the family's mailman and friend as he dropped me off just a few short blocks from the hotel where I was to meet Sam. This giving me the opportunity to gather my thoughts and to calm down my insides as I believe there were butterflies fluttering around in there. Knowing my entire life would soon change, there were a lot of thoughts and emotions running through my mind and heart. With whatever the future has in store for me; only God himself knew this and would guide me on my new life's journey.

Entering the door of the hotel, I looked around and only a few people had occupied the lobby. As I seated myself now on a cushioned chair in the lobby of the hotel, I watched people as they came and went. With every person that came through the front doors, I looked up with my heart fluttering, just waiting and watching for Sam to enter the hotel. Letting out a sigh, when it wouldn't be him, yet my heart beating fast and with what I thought was loud for even others in the hotel to hear, but it was only me. Only I could hear my heart, beating loudly like a rhythmical drum. As the minutes slowly ticked by; I waited patiently. Feeling as ready as I would ever be, waiting for Sam. It was as if time as we know it, had just stood still as the hotel doors opened once more and in through those doors walked a man. A tall lean man, yet muscular in his build. Remembering now, Sam 's photograph, this was the man whom I had written many letters to, as well as receiving the many letters written by him. This man was Sam, the man that I had long awaited to meet and now, was soon to become his wife.

Sam, glancing around the hotel, had seen me sitting there waiting patiently. He recognized me as well, by my photo and began walking my way. Even though, he felt he knew who I was, it was polite to ask if I was Sarah, the woman in the photo that he had held up. Replying softly, I also said his name out loud, yet only loud enough for Sam to hear, as the words were spoken softly. Once we had gotten that out of the way, he took a seat next to me and we talked for quite a while. Reminiscing over our letters to each other and telling each other of our families. Conversation came easily for the two of us, and that, in itself was very relaxing. Thinking back, just moments earlier of how nervous I thought it would be when we first met. *(Would Sam, like what he saw; this woman in person as opposed to the woman in the pictures that had been mailed to him, months before).* Though, I hadn't really changed any, still the same person as the one in the photo. To me, Sam looked pretty much the same. He was tall and had a slender build. He definitely was recognizable from his photo. Being grateful for this time we had together, being able to talk the way we did. It had given me a sense of comfort and it was relaxing to be around him.

We passed the time for at least a good hour, maybe a bit more. Seeing now, what the time it had come to be, we headed for the door of the hotel. Sam, gently placing his hand in the small of my back, as if he were guiding me towards our new journey in life. For me, I was filled with excitement and happiness. Smiling up at him as we walked through the doors. Let our journey begin, as it begins now with the two of us being joined today, together as one.

Approaching now the steps to the city's courthouse, we took each step as if, it they were our very first. The inside of the courthouse was rustic looking yet being very well polished. Finding the information center, we were directed to the room where we were to wait for the Judge who was to perform the ceremony. Approaching the room now where we would soon say our vows of marriage to each other, we continued with soft spoken conversation while we sat in wait. Entering the room, were two people, thinking that maybe they were witnesses that would be signing our marriage certificate. It was a quaint room, and the sun filtered in through the windows, as if to warm up the almost empty and very quiet room. Only moments seemed to have passed by and the judge, he entered the room, giving us a faint smile, as if in approval of our day. He was a short and stocky man, with graying in his jet-black hair. His features were stern and serious, though there was a gentleness in his eyes. As he sat himself in his honors' chair, Sam and I then took our place to sit in the front row bench until we were called upon.

THE VOW

Our ceremony was short and sweet. The judge was very pleasant, as he spoke to Sam and I. There in attendance, of course was himself, the Judge, and two others as witnesses to our quiet and memorable ceremony. Though it was a day to remember because it was our special day. The day Sam and I became husband and wife.

It may not have been even an hour, and all the proceedings were finished, and Sam and I were now, husband and wife. I kept saying that phrase over and over again in my head. It had finally happened, this day of ours. It had a nice ring to it, that phrase. Sam and I couldn't be happier with each other, as we were on that very special day.

It was decided that before we head back to the house, that I had grew up in; to pick up my suitcases; only having three of them; Sam and I would walk just a few blocks to have lunch at a quaint little diner. It felt different somehow, walking with this man; that was now my husband. Me, no longer feeling like I didn't belong anywhere, for now I did belong, I was Sam 's wife and that brought a wonderful feeling. Sam was a bit older than myself, though that didn't matter to either one of us. For what we had shared in our letters, we could also share with each other in person. It would be a growing and learning process for both of us, and this is a journey we were committed to take together.

After our lunch together at the diner, we walked back to the hotel and registered as husband and wife. Telling the clerk, we would soon return and then strolled out the front door. We had approached Sam 's car and being a most courteous gentleman and husband, he held open the car door for me, and I graciously took my place in his vehicle. We soon were on our way, to pick up my suitcases that I had left waiting for me, by my bedroom door. As we drove, we talked of our future plans and of my meeting his family. Of course, I was nervous, who wouldn't be.

A NEW LIFE BEGINS

The ride itself, didn't seem to take awfully long. It may have just seemed that way. Sam and I were talking quite easily to each other. I guess, I first had felt that maybe I wouldn't know what to say, or maybe even know how to say it. Though conversation seemed to come naturally and that, I think helped to put both of us more at ease. Just as the words came easily when I first began writing Sam. Now with Sam driving, I felt very much at ease for the most part, what I mean is that being very much a newlywed, there were still butterflies, but they were all incredibly good butterflies.

We had arrived at the home of my parents, and I had given Sam a glance and a faint smile. He knew of my nervousness, and his presence helped put me at ease. Everything was going to be alright. Pulling into the long dirt driveway, I could see no one about the yard. My father at this time of the day would certainly be in the field and uncertain where my mother would be. Making brief conversation with Sam, I would be returning shortly, with only a few belongings and we once again would be on our way.

Stepping inside my once family home, it felt very strange, it all seemed very different now, with my being here. Remembering only a few hours ago, I was walking out, and now I am walking in. Feeling almost empty inside, my memories taking me back in what felt like a lifetime ago. Then with the feeling of a warm touch to my shoulder, I turned around to find Sam standing behind me, with a warm and comforting smile. I nodded, and knew I needed to gather the few things that we had come here for. Only being a moment, I went to what was once my room in this house and gathered up the few suitcases that I had already packed. Taking a slow look around the room, I knew deep down that I would miss this place called home. It was a feeling of bittersweet, and yet knowing this is what and how it needed to be.

With the one suitcase under my arm and carrying the other two, I stepped into the living room which was directly connected to the kitchen. Couldn't help to take one last look at how things looked here. Keeping this memory in my mind forever.

The letters that I had written my Father and Mother, were still propped up on the kitchen table. Knowing for sure that they would be found. I would write them once again, after I got settled in. I knew in my heart that Papa would be sad but would also understand. My Mother, I was feeling a lot of mixed emotions and just wasn't certain in my heart how she would feel. Time would only tell as the days would pass, just as the sun would rise and set, so would my thoughts and feelings.

OUR JOURNEY

Sam waited so patiently for me, while I said my final goodbyes to this once home of mine. Stepping out onto the front porch with the few belongings I had, taking a long glance around, yet not seeing my parents anywhere in sight, a look of sadness had overtaken my being. I had my memories, and I did have my pictures. Though was still hoping to catch even a glimpse of either one of them, before I left, and I was on my way to create a life for myself and with Sam by my side.

Waiting just a few moments, and still not seeing either one of them, I started slowly down the few steps that we had with my few belongings, we would soon be on our way.

Even though I felt utterly happy, there was still an aching sadness in leaving. Trying not to dwell on that, I would keep in touch with my Father and my Mother, even if it needed to be through letters. With this thought, Sam was putting my suitcases in the car and had waited patiently for me to take my place in the vehicle that would take us to our new home.

Moving now, slowly down the long dirt driveway, that would take us on our new journey home. A home that would be built by the two of us and the family that we would start together.

The snow had nearly melted, with only small patches that lay now in scattered areas in the neighboring fields. Spring would soon come and even nature would make her own changes. Knowing now, or I believe I somehow always did, time changes everything. Some changes a person seems never to be aware of, until it actually happens. I guess that's just the way it is. So, to take it for what it is; as some changes aren't bad changes, they're just changes. Does that make sense, I think it will if you really stop and think about it, tomorrow is a new day, with new beginnings.

It was relaxing now, as we drove away from the old homestead. When we arrived at the hotel, it had become a busy place. There were many people waiting in line, to be checked into a room. We were at ease knowing that we already had a room for the night and would begin our journey back to Sam 's home in the morning. Which was soon to be called our home.

LIFE UNFOLDS

The sun rose early, just as Sam and I had. Wanting to get an early start with our day, with everything packed between us, we were once again on our way. Checking out of the hotel, we put our belongs into the car, and strolled down to the local café'. It was nice to be seated across from this man who I now call my husband. It had a nice ring about it, and I repeated this over and over again in my head. It sounded like a fairy tale, though this was no fairy tale. Everything about it, was as real as real could be. We enjoyed having our early breakfast just about as much as we enjoyed each other's conversation.

We were once again, on our way. On our way to going home. My home now would be with Sam. We would settle into his parent's home, only until Sam would be able to get us a home of our own. We talked about my meeting his family, and he reassured me that everything would be fine. He somehow, seemed to know that I was definitely feeling nervous and a little apprehensive, yet I would have faith, faith in him to settle any uneasy feelings that would want to overtake me. So, not letting those feelings wash me out, I began to relax, at least for now.

We drove for a long time, though it really didn't feel that long at all. The scenery was just beautiful to look at. I remembered the last time I viewed any scenery was when I had taken the bus trip to Aunt and Uncle's in Oklahoma. This seemed different, maybe it was because I was older, or at least that's what it felt like. Though now, I was with Sam and it felt wonderful to be with him. This was all so very new to me, though I didn't, in any way feel uneasy or afraid. It was like, this is where I was meant to be.

We drove till nearly dark and found a place to stay for the night. We would continue our journey in the morning. We didn't have all that much further to go. We would arrive at the home of Sam 's parents sometime that next day.

We, of course made our stops along the way. To see a few sights and for eating, otherwise we drove almost non-stop. The time just seemed to roll right by. Enjoying our time together, was the best. Getting to know each other as the minutes turned in to hours, then into the days that would lead us both home.

FAMILY TIME

With the drive nearly now behind us, we were coming into the city of where Sam lived. Nervousness seemed to settle in again. Sam could see this by the look on my face. Reassuring me that his family knew of me and of how much I meant to him. They were expecting us, and everything would be okay. Though his words were trying to put me at ease, I still felt nervous. Though, who wouldn't be, meeting my husbands' family. It was one thing, finally meeting him and that in itself was wonderful. Yet now I was to meet his family, there were so many thoughts running through my head, I could hardly keep up with them all. Taking a deep breath and making sure I looked alright, we stepped into the home of his family.

His home was filled with so many people. My goodness, what a reception. Sam said his hello's and then introduced me to his family. It did, kind of take me by surprise, I was greeted with such a warm welcome. It was almost as if, they had already known me, and that I wasn't at all a stranger to them. Their greetings and welcoming did make me feel more at ease. More at ease, then what I was feeling only moments before.

Getting settled in just a bit. There was an awfully good meal waiting for us. They had gone to great lengths preparing such an abundance of food. Everything looked and smelled wonderful.

The atmosphere was getting more comfortable as the time passed. I felt more at ease now, then I had in the beginning. Sam could sense this, so I knew that this was more comfortable for him too. Sam 's family was very pleasant to me and made me feel very welcomed.

I didn't know just how much they knew about me, or what all Sam had told them. With whatever they knew, they didn't ask too many questions, which I was feeling incredibly grateful for. Things would unfold as time passed, and I wasn't in any hurry to reveal too much, too soon, or maybe not at all.

Maybe, it would be, that I wouldn't have to explain or say too much at any one given time. I would leave things as they were.

The afternoon turned into early evening and this reception get together turned out to be quite nice. Making myself useful, I helped with the cleanup of this big meal that was prepared for us. It was a good feeling, to be welcomed into Sam 's family.

ON OUR OWN

It was soon feeling more like Spring and the weather was getting to be quite nice. Sam and I, we ultimately had our own home. Even though it was in his parent's back yard, it was still ours. As this was to be temporary, it was ours. Ours to make into a home of our own as we began to have a family of our own.

It was just a few months after our permanent home was built, that I had received a letter from my mother. With trembling fingers and unsteady hands, I apprehensively opened the letter. I needed to read it twice as it was nothing like I had expected. Wasn't sure what it was that I was expecting, but it was a heartwarming letter. My mother was missing me and was wishing me the absolute best. She was hoping that I and my family would be able to come for a visit sometime.

I guess over time, time can change people and they seem to soften. Leaving behind the bitterness and maybe even anger. I would call this softening of the heart, as this would having a calming effect of a persons' being. Receiving the letter from her made my heart feel a sense of relief and contentment.

As the years passed, they seemed to have gone by ever so quickly. Like the seasons changing, the years were changing just that same way. With having now, our permanent home, our family was growing, we continued to grow together and as a family. It was as if it were a photo book of family memories, we could all cherish.

The days that followed turned into months and the years seem to give way to what we call time. So much has happened, so many things and more importantly we had a world filled with memories. Not all the memories that we had were the best. As with many other couples, there were heartaches and pain. Though, they were ours alone, ours to expand on and even to build on. As we grew together in our married life, our children were also growing into young adults. As they soon would begin to have lives of their own. This would become as a memory photo album of the lives that we lived.

A HEARTACHE IN TIME

So many unexpected turns in life, with so many things that have happened over the years. That in, itself feels like nearly a lifetime ago. These memories will be cherished in what I will call 'My Forever'. Then there are those that not just myself alone, but I would guess to say, there could be others that anyone would like to not remember. Though, that's not how life goes, they will always be there.

Now with my children all grown and having families of their own, it was just my beloved Sam and myself. Sam by this time was retired from his job of nearly 30 some years. We lived through

222

some hard times, though we made it over the obstacles that we encountered. This had made each of us stronger. With our growing family and most of all with each other.

Sometimes I wonder where my life would have ended up if it were not for Sam coming into my life. Can't even imagine life now without him. Don't want to dwell on what could have been, that is no longer a part of my life. There is no time for what ifs. My life is what has happened the first day Sam and I had started exchanging letters. That is, what is most important to me and all that matters, is what is now.

How does anyone explain the pain in another one's heart? No one could even begin to imagine the sadness that lies there. Oh, I guess you could try, though I don't think you could unless you have traveled a road so lonely and there is no one waiting at the other end to catch you if you fall. Though, for me there were so many people, my family, my children, and even close friends to catch me, when I lost my Sam. I have never felt so sad, so alone. Sam was my whole world. Sure, I had my children, though it wasn't the same as losing the only love of your life. We spent sixty years together, he and I. He was my first love and now he will always be my only. My heart felt so fragile now and oh so empty. Feeling like my heart was made of glass, and now it has been shattered.

Feeling like I was living in a shadow of myself. Going through the motions and putting on a smile when it was needed. Yes, there were still good memories to be made, yet they would be without Sam, my life would continue until I someday again will be joined with the love of my life. Yet, there still lies such an emptiness that it was nearly too difficult to explain. Maybe the days ahead would get a little easier, though I would do my best to live out the rest of my life, being there for my children. The children that I loved and raised with Sam.

A person will always have a piece or sometimes many pieces of someone, whom is so dearly missed. As my children will always have pieces of their father and of me. Think about how short a life really is. Always remember and carry them with you no matter where your life may take you. If you don't have memories than you may be lost. Searching for something you may never find if you're not making memories that you will always carry with you.

HE IS WAITING

This part of anyone's story can be a bit difficult. Though I will do my best and share what I can and or what I know. So much has happened over the years, some were the most wonderful and of course, there were some that were full of heartache. I guess that is what memories are, right? A person lives as best they can with what they have been given. It's all up to us to take it and do the very best with it. Not saying, that there won't be mistakes along the way, and wishing at times things could have been different. Though, thinking this is what makes us who we are, and even where we are headed, when we act on the good thoughts of what it was; that we had been thinking.

At times, I still feel so very empty inside, missing Sam every day. My children, I know love me and some show it in many ways, while others seem to keep a certain distance from me. I look for them sometimes and they are not here. I will always love them, and I wonder if they even know just how much. Some things, only if you are a mother would understand. Though there are fathers, that have gone through so many similar things and they too can feel the loss and uncertainties of their families.

It was at a time during my later years in life when I no longer was able to stay alone in my home. Having the love and care of one of my daughters, every day was always a blessing. With my other children coming to visit and with them and their help, more memories were created. I was and would be forever grateful. With loving my children, each one at times would help where the others weren't able. Sam and I also had a son, who was so much like his father. Sam would be and I know is so enormously proud of you, as I know I am. Each one holding a very special piece of my heart, this is for them.

As the months passed, I had become saddened by the things that I used to do. The things that had once kept me busy, and pleased my heart, I now could no longer do. This was a feeling that is nearly too difficult to put into words. It sure made my heart sad and with thoughts of what lie ahead had taken over my most inner thoughts and feelings. Bringing back so many memories of all the many things that I had learned as a child, and then as a wife and even now as a mother.

I know that no one knows how their life will end when that day comes. We are not supposed to know. Yet, it makes a person wonder, how did I ever end up here? Even though the answers may lie before us, as our days have already unfolded, the thoughts still persist, and we still ask the questions.

As the days turned into weeks, my health was failing, even more now, and I knew my time would come soon. I knew what was happening to me, as did my children. My daughters were here to help care for me as best they could. I couldn't tell them, though I knew in my heart that they knew what it meant to have them here.

I lay here now in and out of awareness, searching for the memories that brought me here. Reflecting now, to near the beginning of when I first became physically and emotionally aware of this young woman that had looked back at me from the mirror that one early day so long ago. As it now felt like such a lifetime ago, in the home that I had grown up in as a child.

There was this young woman looking into this mirror, a mirror of life now, if you will. Looking back at me, I now see her and now behind her I am seeing the woman that I had grown up to be. Oh! Those memories between those two women and how far they had come in this life. Seeing this woman was like looking into a mirrored soul. Now it was a mirror of time. I see both of them now, the young child and the woman she had become. This woman she has lived a full life and would soon be with the love of her life. Her Sam, her first love and her only love. I'll be home soon my dearest.

HEAVEN'S EARTH ANGEL

As I lay here, my body slowly dies. Yet, my soul is alive and seeks the face of God

My mind, when at rest; plays out my life and the many blessings I've been given.

Though in anguish, I feel the angel of mercy protecting me and shielding me from the pain; the pain in which my body has been burdened to bear

As the hours pass into days, I lie in wait. Lord I don't know how much longer I can keep doing this. Why is this taking so long?

Lord, I know you will not forsake me, please open the doors of Heaven and let me walk in to embrace you.

I have been told that I am an Earth Angel. This does bring a smile to my heart. Dear Lord: I give of myself to you, and I am ready

Jesus, I'm coming home

As my children live on, please guide them, keep them, and give each of them the strength that I have found in you

Comfort them when their hearts are heavy

Carry them when their weary bodies are weak

Let the tears that fall; be tears of joy

for my life

Not tears of sadness for me and the

things that once was

For memories that live on; that I might

bring smiles to their faces when they

remember me

My Earthly Angel Days have come to

pass

I have now become an Angel of Heaven

Adorned by You

Blessed by you

An Earthly Angel that has now been

given wings

www.ingramcontent.com/pod-product-compliance
Lightning Source LLC
Chambersburg PA
CBHW021240260626
47155CB00004BA/1238